CW01176054

"Cosmic Horizon Collection"

2, Volume 2

Anthony Fontenot

Published by Anthony Fontenot, 2024.

Cosmic Starlight Odyssey
And
Cosmic Horizon
And
Merging

By Anthony Fontenot

© Anthony Fontenot

This is a work of fiction. Similarities to real people, places, or events are entirely coincidental.

"COSMIC HORIZON COLLECTION"

First edition. November 18, 2024.

Copyright © 2024 Anthony Fontenot.

ISBN: 979-8230118459

Written by Anthony Fontenot.

It hasn't been easy finding my right audience but if you're reading this, hard work does pay off and I'm glad you're reading my book. Thank you. Hope you enjoy this adventurous journey you're about to embark on

Thank you to my Dad Toney and stepmom Beth

Congratulations Jessica. I'm excited for the new addition to our family. It's been a great year. I can't think my readers enough thank you thank you thank you.....

Thank you

To my readers I really do appreciate you

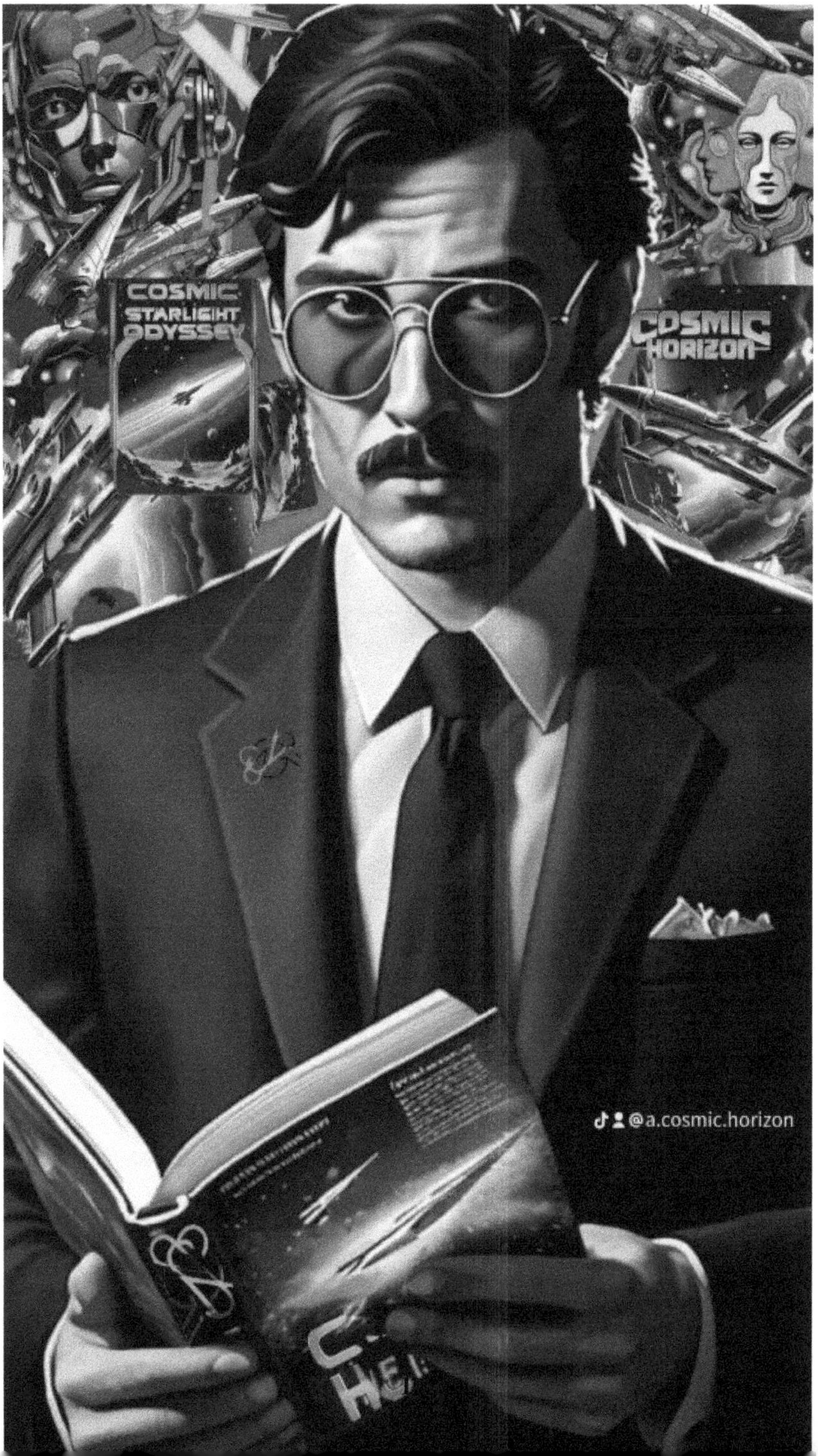
COSMIC
STARLIGHT
ODYSSEY
COSMIC
HORIZON
@a.cosmic.horizon

All available

"COSMIC HORIZON COLLECTION"

in this book

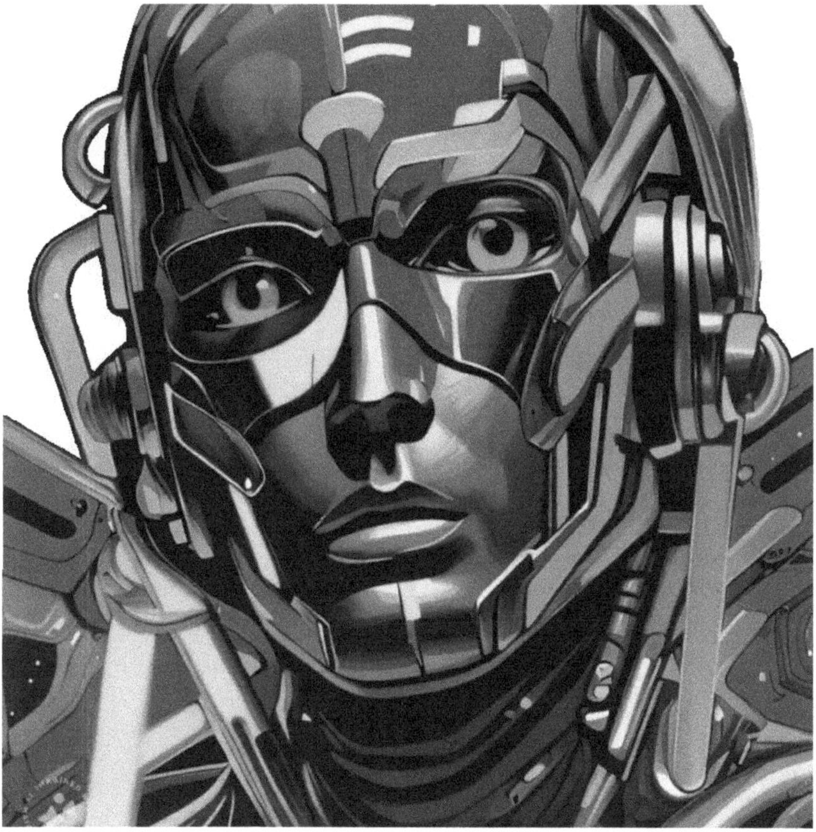

ANTHONY FONTENOT

Starlight Odyssey

Chapter 1: The Cosmic Horizon

Humanity stood at the threshold of a new era, venturing deeper into the cosmos. Stars and galaxies beckoned, promising secrets and mysteries beyond imagination. But amidst the wonder, a threat lurked – the spread of

Fabricated stories and hoaxes threatened to undermine humanity's understanding of the universe. Powerful interests exploited the chaos, spreading false information through sophisticated algorithms. Public opinion was manipulated, and trust began to erode.

In response, the Cosmic Truth Initiative emerged, a coalition of intergalactic organizations united in their quest for fact-based information. Their mission was clear: promote critical thinking, develop cutting-edge misinformation detection tools, and foster a culture of transparency.

The forces of misinformation would not go quietly into the night. Agents of disinformation launched counterattacks, seeking to discredit the Cosmic Truth Initiative. But the advocates of truth stood firm, deploying AI-driven fact-checking bots and whistleblower protection programs. The battle for cosmic integrity had begun.

Chapter 2: The Web of Deceit

Agent Rachel Kim's eyes narrowed as she scrutinized Julian Saint Clair's every word. His revelation about the Echo Protocol had raised more questions than answers.

"What makes you think the Syndicate is after the Echo Protocol?" Rachel asked, her tone measured.

Julian leaned back, steepling his fingers. "I've seen classified documents. The Syndicate believes the Echo Protocol can amplify their control over cosmic frequencies, manipulating the fabric of space-time itself."

Rachel's mind raced. "And what's your role in this?"

Julian's gaze turned enigmatic. "Let's just say I have... motivations. Help me stop the Syndicate, and I'll ensure you get the truth."

Rachel hesitated, weighing the risks. Could she trust Julian?

Suddenly, her comms device beeped. "Agent Kim, we've detected unusual energy signatures near the Syndicate's HQ."

Rachel's instincts kicked in. "Looks like our move. Julian, you're coming with me."

As they approached the Syndicate's HQ, Rachel could feel the air thickening with tension. Julian's presence by her side was both reassuring and unsettling.

Upon arrival, they discovered a hidden entrance, guarded by elite agents.

"Julian, recognize anyone?" Rachel whispered.

Julian's eyes locked onto a familiar face. "That's Victor LaGrange. My... acquaintance."

Victor's gaze snapped toward Julian, his expression a mix of surprise and hostility.

"Julian Saint Clair. I didn't think you'd dare show your face here."

Rachel's grip on her blaster tightened. "This isn't a reunion. We're here for the Echo Protocol."

Victor sneered. "You're too late. The Protocol is already activated."

Rachel's eyes locked onto Victor. "What do you mean the Echo Protocol is activated?"

Victor's smile grew wider. "The Syndicate has harnessed its power. Cosmic frequencies are now under our control."

Julian's face darkened. "You fool, Victor. You don't understand the consequences."

Victor shrugged. "Consequences are for the weak. We'll reshape the cosmos in our image."

Rachel knew time was running out. "We need to shut down the Protocol."

Julian nodded. "I can guide you through the facility, but we'll face heavy resistance."

As they infiltrated the stronghold, blaster fire erupted around them. Syndicate agents closed in.

Chapter 3: The Heart of the Stronghold

Navigating through the labyrinthine corridors, Julian led Rachel to the Protocol's core.

"The Echo Protocol's energy signature is destabilizing the cosmos," Julian warned.

Rachel's determination hardened. "We'll stop this, no matter the cost."

Inside the core, they found the source of the energy signature: a massive crystal pulsating with cosmic energy.

Victor appeared, flanked by elite agents. "You'll never leave this place alive."

Rachel and Julian exchanged a glance. This was their last stand.

Rachel and Julian fought for survival, surrounded by Victor's elite agents.

"We need to disable the Protocol!" Rachel shouted.

"I'll try to hack the crystal's frequency!" Julian yelled back, returning fire.

The agents closed in, their blasters unleashing a hail of deadly bolts.

"We're outnumbered!" Rachel warned.

"Hold on!" Julian replied. "Almost there!"

Just as all seemed lost, the facility's alarms blared. The lights flickered.

"What's happening?" Rachel yelled.

"The Protocol's collapsing!" Julian shouted. "We have to get out!"

The room shook as the crystal's energy surged. Agents stumbled, disoriented.

"Now's our chance! Move!" Rachel ordered.

Together, they fought their way through the chaos.

Victor, enraged, lunged at Rachel. "You'll pay for this!"

Julian intervened, taking down the Syndicate leader. "Not today, Victor."

As they escaped the crumbling facility, Rachel turned to Julian. "We did it. The Protocol's down."

Julian's gaze lingered on the destruction. "This isn't over. The Syndicate will regroup."

Rachel's determination hardened. "We'll be ready. What's next?"

Julian's eyes locked onto hers. "Meet me on planet Nixxar. We have unfinished business."

Rachel's comms device beeped. "Agent Kim, report to HQ. Debriefing awaits."

"Understood," Rachel replied.

Julian's message followed: "Nixxar, Rachel. Don't forget."

Rachel's thoughts swirled with questions.

"Julian, what's on Nixxar?" she asked.

"Answers," Julian replied. "And more questions."

Rachel's agency director, Commander Patel, greeted her at HQ.

"Agent Kim, congrats on stopping the Protocol. But we have concerns."

"What kind?" Rachel asked.

"Rumors of a rogue agent within our ranks," Patel revealed. "And whispers of a hidden Syndicate faction."

Rachel's eyes narrowed. "I'll investigate."

Patel nodded. "Be careful, Agent Kim. The stakes are higher than ever."

Rachel's investigation into the rogue agent led her to a secluded sector of the agency's database. She uncovered a cryptic message:

"Project Elysium: Eyes only. Authorized personnel."

Rachel's curiosity piqued, she accessed the file.

"Project Elysium" revealed a shocking truth: the agency had secretly collaborated with the Syndicate to develop the Echo Protocol.

Rachel's stomach churned. "Who authorized this?"

A name caught her eye: Agent Thompson, her trusted colleague.

Rachel's comms device beeped. "Agent Kim, meet me on Nixxar."

Julian's message.

"Julian, I've found something," Rachel replied. "Project Elysium. Our agency's involved."

Julian's response was immediate. "I knew it. Meet me ASAP."

Rachel arrived on Nixxar, her mind reeling with questions.

Julian greeted her, his expression grim. "Rachel, we have a mole."

"Agent Thompson," Rachel revealed.

Julian nodded. "I suspected as much. Thompson's been feeding intel to the Syndicate."

Rachel's anger flared. "We need to bring them down."

Julian handed her a data pad. "Evidence is here. But we need more."

Their mission clear, they set out to gather proof and take down the rogue agents.

As they navigated the complex web of deceit, Rachel and Julian encountered unexpected allies and foes.

"Who can we trust?" Rachel asked.

Julian's gaze locked onto hers. "Each other. That's all we have."

Their bond strengthened, they forged ahead, determined to expose the truth.

But the Syndicate wouldn't go down without a fight.

Agent Thompson's betrayal cut deep. Rachel struggled to reconcile the colleague she thought she knew with the traitor before her.

"Why, Thompson?" Rachel demanded.

Thompson sneered. "The Syndicate promised power, resources... a new order."

Julian's eyes narrowed. "And what about our agency's director, Commander Patel?"

Thompson's smile grew wider. "Patel's been playing both sides. Syndicate loyalist, agency director... the perfect mole."

Rachel's world crumbled. Her trusted leader, a traitor?

Julian's grip on her arm steadied her. "We'll take them down, together."

Their mission clear, they infiltrated the agency's high-security facility.

Confronting Commander Patel, Rachel's emotions simmered.

"Sir, we have evidence," Rachel stated, her voice firm.

Patel's expression remained calm. "Evidence of what, Agent Kim?"

"Your ties to the Syndicate," Julian accused.

Patel's facade crumbled. "You're too late. The Syndicate's already in control."

Rachel's anger boiled over. "Not while I'm still breathing."

In a tense standoff, Rachel and Julian apprehended Patel.

As they escorted the director away, Rachel vowed, "Justice will be served."

But the Syndicate's grip remained strong.

Chapter 4: The Shadow Syndicate

In the shadows, Victor's successor, the enigmatic Archon, orchestrated the Syndicate's resurgence.

"Patel's fall is merely a setback," Archon declared. "Our true plan unfolds."

A mysterious figure emerged from the darkness.

"And what of Rachel Kim and Julian Saint Clair?" the figure asked.

Archon's smile sent chills down the figure's spine. "They'll soon learn the true meaning of power."

The stakes escalated. Rachel and Julian faced a revitalized enemy.

Archon's plan unfolded like a sinister tapestry. Rachel and Julian, now hunted by the Syndicate, fled to the underworld of Nixxar's shadowy districts.

"We need allies," Julian urged. "The Syndicate's too powerful."

Rachel nodded. "I know someone. Meet me at Club Erebus."

In the dimly lit club, they found Rachel's contact, the enigmatic smuggler, Phoenix.

"Phoenix, we need your help," Rachel requested.

Phoenix's gaze lingered on Julian. "What's in it for me?"

Julian smiled. "Access to Syndicate tech. Worth a fortune."

Phoenix nodded. "Deal. But I have conditions."

As they negotiated, Archon's agents closed in.

A traitor within Phoenix's ranks revealed their location. Syndicate forces stormed Club Erebus.

"Traitor!" Phoenix spat, executing the mole.

Rachel and Julian fought alongside Phoenix's crew, but they were outnumbered.

In the chaos, Julian disappeared.

"Julian!" Rachel screamed.

Phoenix grabbed her arm. "We must retreat. Now."

Rachel hesitated, then followed Phoenix.

Chapter 5: The Lost Operative

Rachel's search for Julian led her to the darkest corners of Nixxar.

"Julian, respond!" Rachel pleaded over comms.

Silence.

Days passed. Rachel's hope dwindled.

Then, a message:

"Meet me at sector 7. Come alone."

Julian's voice.

Rachel's heart skipped a beat.

Rachel arrived at sector 7, gun drawn.

Julian emerged from shadows, his eyes haunted.

"Rachel, I've been playing both sides," Julian confessed. "Syndicate and agency. I had to."

Rachel's world crumbled. "Why?"

Julian's gaze locked onto hers. "To protect you. The Syndicate wants you dead."

Rachel's trust wavered.

Rachel's eyes narrowed. "Why does the Syndicate want me dead, Julian?"

Julian hesitated. "Your past, Rachel. It's more complicated than you think."

Rachel's grip on her blaster tightened. "Tell me."

Julian's voice dropped to a whisper. "You were part of a secret program, codenamed 'Eclipse.' The Syndicate wants to exploit your unique skills."

Rachel's memories began to resurface.

"Eclipse... I remember fragments. Training, enhancements... and something went wrong."

Julian nodded. "The program was shut down, but the Syndicate revived it. They need your expertise for their plans."

Rachel's determination hardened. "I won't let them."

Archon addressed his inner circle. "Rachel Kim's Eclipse training makes her a valuable asset. Capture her, and we'll control the cosmos."

A hooded figure stepped forward. "I'll handle it."

The figure revealed: Agent Vega, Rachel's former Eclipse colleague.

"Vega, why?" Rachel asked, shocked.

Vega's gaze turned cold. "Loyalty, Rachel. To the Syndicate, and to ourselves."

The Eclipse program's dark secrets began to unravel.

Vega's revelation shook Rachel. "You're with the Syndicate?"

Vega's expression remained cold. "I adapted, Rachel. Eclipse trained us to survive."

Rachel's anger flared. "At what cost? Innocent lives?"

Vega shrugged. "Collateral damage. The Syndicate promises power, protection."

Rachel's determination hardened. "I won't join you, Vega."

Vega sneered. "You'll come willingly or by force."

Archon's voice echoed through the comms system. "Agent Vega, bring Rachel Kim alive."

Vega's team moved to surround Rachel.

Julian appeared, blaster blazing. "Not today, Vega."

Vega's eyes narrowed. "Julian Saint Clair. Traitor."

Julian fought alongside Rachel, taking down Vega's team.

As they escaped, Rachel confronted Julian. "Why did you help me?"

Julian's gaze locked onto hers. "Loyalty, Rachel. To you, not the Syndicate."

Rachel's trust wavered, but she saw sincerity in Julian's eyes.

Chapter 6: Hidden Agenda

In a secure hideout, Phoenix awaited them.

"Phoenix, what's your stake in this?" Rachel asked.

Phoenix leaned in. "Archon's plan threatens my operations. I want him taken down."

Julian's eyes narrowed. "What's Archon's plan?"

Phoenix hesitated. "Ancient technology... hidden on planet Arkeia."

Rachel's instincts flared. "What technology?"

Phoenix's voice dropped to a whisper. "A device capable of controlling the cosmos."

The stakes escalated.

Rachel's eyes widened. "A device controlling the cosmos? That's impossible."

Phoenix nodded. "Archon believes it's key to the Syndicate's dominance."

Julian's gaze turned calculating. "We need to get to Arkeia first."

Phoenix handed them a data pad. "Coordinates and intel. Be careful."

Rachel's determination hardened. "We won't let Archon control the cosmos."

On Arkeia, they navigated treacherous landscapes and ancient ruins.

Julian scanned their surroundings. "Energy signatures ahead."

Rachel drew her blaster. "Let's move."

Inside the ancient temple, they discovered cryptic artifacts and murals.

Vega's voice echoed through comms. "Rachel, surrender. Archon's patience wears thin."

Rachel's response was firm. "Never."

Chapter 7: The Device

Deep within the temple, they found the device: an orb pulsing with cosmic energy.

Julian's eyes locked onto the orb. "This is it. The key to controlling the cosmos."

Rachel's grip on her blaster tightened. "We can't let Archon have it."

Suddenly, the temple shook. Archon's forces breached the temple.

"Take the orb!" Archon ordered.

Vega and her team closed in.

Rachel aimed her blaster, firing at Vega's team. "Cover Julian!"

Julian sprinted toward the orb, dodging blaster fire.

Vega sneered. "You'll never escape!"

Rachel returned fire, taking down several agents.

Julian reached the orb, but Archon appeared, blaster pressed to Julian's head.

"Hand it over, Julian," Archon demanded.

Rachel's heart sank.

With a fierce cry, Rachel launched herself at Archon.

Blaster fire erupted around them.

Julian seized the distraction, tossing the orb to Rachel.

She caught it, feeling its energy course through her.

Archon's eyes widened. "No!"

Rachel fired her blaster point-blank at Archon.

The Syndicate leader stumbled back, wounded.

Vega's team retreated.

As the dust settled, Rachel helped Julian up.

"Thanks for the save," Julian said.

Rachel smiled grimly. "We're even."

The orb pulsed brighter, responding to Rachel's touch.

"What does it do?" Julian asked.

Rachel's eyes locked onto the orb. "I think it's connected to my Eclipse enhancements."

Suddenly, the temple began to destabilize.

"We need to get out – now!" Julian warned.

As they escaped the crumbling temple, Rachel pondered the orb's secrets.

"What's Phoenix's true motive?" Rachel asked.

Julian's gaze turned calculating. "Phoenix has ties to an ancient organization, hidden for centuries."

Rachel's eyes widened. "What organization?"

"The Order of the Nova," Julian revealed. "They seek balance in the cosmos."

Phoenix's voice echoed through comms. "Well done, Rachel. The orb's safe."

Rachel's distrust flared. "What's your stake in this, Phoenix?"

Phoenix hesitated. "I'm an Order agent. My mission: protect the orb from those who'd misuse its power."

Chapter 8: Nova's Agenda

At the Order's hidden base, Phoenix introduced Rachel and Julian to Nova's leader, Astrid.

Astrid's eyes shone with determination. "The orb's power can bring harmony or chaos. We must ensure its safekeeping."

Rachel's grip on the orb tightened. "I won't let it fall into Syndicate hands."

Astrid nodded. "We'll help you master the orb's energy."

Julian's gaze lingered on Astrid. "What's the true cost of Nova's protection?"

Astrid's expression turned enigmatic. "Alliances come with sacrifices, Julian."

Under Astrid's guidance, Rachel honed her skills, mastering the orb's energy.

"The orb responds to your Eclipse enhancements," Astrid explained.

Rachel's connection to the orb deepened, unlocking new abilities.

Julian observed, his expression thoughtful. "You're becoming a formidable force, Rachel."

Archon, wounded but determined, rallied the Syndicate.

"Capture Rachel Kim and the orb," Archon ordered. "Crush the Order of the Nova."

Vega led the assault on Nova's base.

Rachel, Julian, and Nova agents defended their stronghold.

The battle raged on.

As Syndicate forces breached the base, Rachel unleashed the orb's full power.

A blinding energy wave repelled the attackers.

Vega stumbled back, her eyes wide. "Impossible!"

Rachel stood firm, the orb's energy coursing through her.

"We won't be intimidated," Rachel declared.

Archon's voice echoed through comms. "You may have won this battle, but the war is far from over." The stakes escalated.

Chapter 9: Aftermath

The battle won, Rachel and Julian assessed the damage.

"Astrid, how bad is it?" Rachel asked.

Astrid's expression was grim. "We lost several agents. Our base is compromised."

Julian nodded. "We need to relocate, regroup."

Rachel's determination hardened. "We won't back down."

Nova's agents relocated to a secure facility.

Rachel began training with the orb, mastering its energy.

Julian worked with Nova's tech experts, analyzing Syndicate intel.

Astrid briefed them on Nova's next move.

"We have a lead on a Syndicate facility," Astrid said. "Intel suggests they're developing a countermeasure to the orb."

Rachel's eyes locked onto Astrid. "We need to infiltrate that facility."

Julian nodded. "I'll get to work on a plan."

Rachel, Julian, and a Nova team infiltrated the Syndicate facility.

They navigated through security systems and guards.

Rachel's orb-enhanced senses guided them.

Inside the lab, they discovered the countermeasure: a device capable of neutralizing the orb's energy.

Vega oversaw the project.

"Welcome, Rachel," Vega sneered. "You're just in time to witness the orb's downfall."

Rachel's grip on the orb tightened. "We can't let you neutralize its power."

Vega sneered. "You're too late. The countermeasure is online."

The device activated, emitting a frequency to disrupt the orb's energy.

Rachel felt the orb's power surging, resisting the countermeasure.

"No!" Vega shouted. "It can't—"

The orb released a blast of energy, overwhelming the device.

The countermeasure exploded, destroying the lab.
Vega stumbled back, shocked.
Rachel stood firm, the orb's energy coursing through her.

STARLIGHT ODYSSEY

Chapter 10: Unleashed

The orb's power spread, infiltrating the facility's systems.

Security systems failed. Alarms silenced.

Rachel, Julian, and the Nova team advanced, unopposed.

Archon's voice echoed through comms. "Vega, report!"

Vega's response was laced with fear. "The orb... it's out of control."

Archon's tone turned cold. "Contain it. At all costs."

The orb's energy continued to spread, disrupting the Syndicate's operations.

Rachel's connection to the orb deepened.

"I won't stop it," Rachel said, determination in her voice.

Julian's eyes locked onto hers. "What's the orb's plan?"

Rachel's gaze turned inward. "I'm not sure. But I trust it."

The orb's energy enveloped the facility, rewriting its infrastructure.

Systems merged, forming an interconnected network.

Rachel's consciousness expanded, becoming one with the orb.

She saw the cosmos, its secrets unfolding before her.

Julian's voice echoed, distant. "Rachel, what's happening?"

Rachel's response was barely audible. "I'm becoming... more."

The orb's power surged, propelling Rachel toward ascension.

Rachel's form began to shift, her molecular structure rearranging.

Her body glowed with an ethereal light, as if infused with stardust.

Julian's eyes widened. "Rachel, no! Don't lose yourself!"

Rachel's voice whispered in his mind. "I'm not losing myself, Julian. I'm finding my true self."

The orb's energy reached its zenith.

Rachel's transformation completed.

She stood tall, a being of cosmic energy.

Rachel's gaze swept the cosmos, perceiving hidden patterns.

Galaxies aligned, their secrets revealed.

The Syndicate's strongholds crumbled, their power broken.

Archon's voice trembled. "Impossible... She's become a—"

Julian finished the thought. "A cosmic entity."

Rachel's voice echoed through the cosmos. "I am the balance. The orb's power, now mine."

Rachel's presence resonated throughout the cosmos, restoring equilibrium.

Stars aligned, planets stabilized, and galaxies harmonized.

The Syndicate's remnants scattered, leaderless.

Archon's voice whispered, defeated. "It's over."

Julian approached Rachel, awe-struck.

"Rachel, you're... radiant."

Rachel's cosmic form smiled.

"I've become what I was meant to be."

cosmic Odyssey

"COSMIC HORIZON COLLECTION" 29

Chapter 11: Nova's Revelation

Astrid appeared, her eyes shining.

"Rachel, you've fulfilled Nova's prophecy."

Rachel's gaze turned inward.

"What prophecy?"

Astrid's voice filled with reverence.

"You are the Celestial Key, unlocking balance in the cosmos."

Rachel's understanding deepened.

"I see. My journey, the orb, it was all leading to this."

Rachel's cosmic form expanded, encompassing the galaxy.

"I will maintain balance, protect the cosmos."

Julian stood beside her, steadfast.

"Together, we'll ensure peace."

Astrid nodded.

"Nova will support you, Rachel. Always."

The cosmos flourished under Rachel's guardianship.

Rachel convened the Celestial Council, gathering cosmic entities.

Ancient beings from distant galaxies attended.

Rachel's presence commanded respect.

"The cosmos needs unity," Rachel declared. "Together, we'll maintain balance."

The council agreed, acknowledging Rachel's leadership.

Under Rachel's guidance, galaxies flourished.

Civilizations prospered, exploring the cosmos.

Julian and Astrid worked alongside Rachel.

Nova's agents became cosmic ambassadors.

The Syndicate's remnants disbanded.

Rachel's legend grew, inspiring generations.

Stars were named after her.

Planets bore her likeness.

Rachel's cosmic form smiled.

"I've created a legacy of balance."

Julian's eyes shone.
"Your legacy will endure."
Astrid nodded.
"Nova's prophecy fulfilled."
Epilogue: Celestial Horizon
Rachel's cosmic form gazed into the horizon.
The cosmos stretched before her.
Endless possibilities awaited.
Rachel's voice whispered.
"I am the Celestial Key."
The galaxy Fade to black.

Chapter 12: Cosmic Fade

The galaxy's vibrant colors dulled.
Stars dimmed, their light extinguished.
Planets cooled, their atmospheres collapsing.
Rachel's cosmic form stood alone.
"The balance is shifting," Rachel whispered.

Cosmic Horizon

Anthony Fontenot

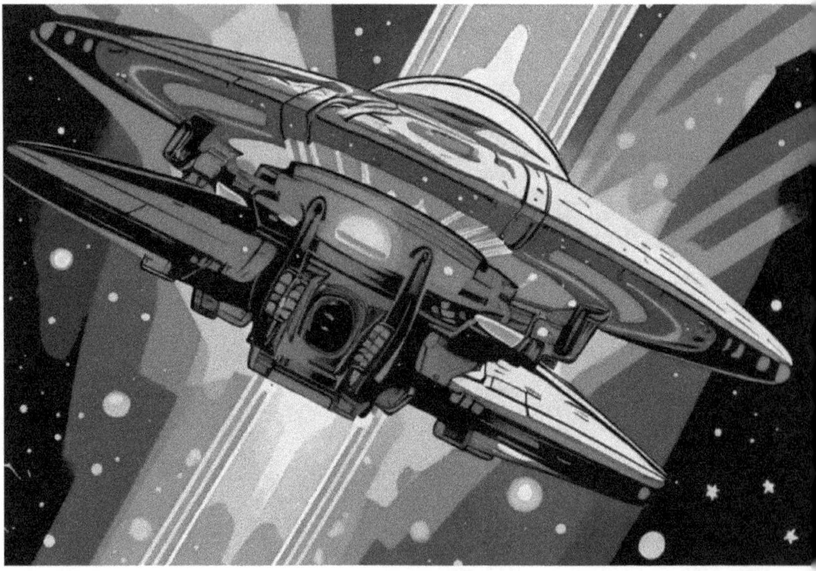

"COSMIC HORIZON COLLECTION"

Julian's voice echoed, distant.
"Rachel, what's happening?"
Rachel's gaze swept the fading galaxy.
"Energy is draining... The cosmos is collapsing."
Astrid's voice trembled.
"Is this the end?"
The void, a vast emptiness, spread.
Galaxies disappeared, consumed.
Rachel's form began to fade.
"I must find the source," Rachel said.
Julian's determination flared.
"We'll find a way to stop this."

Astrid's eyes locked onto Rachel.
"Use the orb's power."
Rachel's cosmic form concentrated.
The orb's energy surged.
Rachel pierced the quantum threshold.
A hidden realm revealed itself.
Ancient entities, architects of the cosmos, awaited.
"You have reached the nexus," they said.
Rachel's determination hardened.
"I won't let the galaxy die."
The architects' response echoed.
"Balance requires sacrifice."
The architects revealed the cosmos' true nature.
"Balance requires renewal," they said.
Rachel's determination hardened.
"I won't let the galaxy die."
The architects presented a choice.
"Sacrifice your cosmic form, Rachel."
Julian's voice trembled.
"Rachel, no!"
Astrid's eyes locked onto Rachel.
"Trust the architects."
Rachel's resolve deepened.
"I'll save the galaxy."
Rachel surrendered her cosmic form.
Energy released, revitalizing the galaxy.
Stars rekindled, planets warmed.
Life burst forth, renewed.
The void receded, its darkness vanquished.
Julian's voice whispered.
"Rachel?"
Astrid's smile shone.

"She's become the galaxy itself."

Epilogue: Eternal Balance

The galaxy flourished, balanced.

Rachel's essence infused every star.

Julian and Astrid roamed the cosmos.

Their hearts carried Rachel's legacy.

The orb, now a beacon, guided civilizations.

In the distance, a whisper echoed.

"I am the galaxy."

Chapter 13: Galactic Rebirth

Rachel's whispered words echoed through the cosmos. "I am the Galaxy."

As her essence infused every molecule, stars pulsed and planets aligned. A new era dawned, and with it, a renewed sense of hope.

Rachel's consciousness expanded, unlocking secrets of the galaxy. Her transformation was complete – she had become one with the cosmos.

"Rachel?" Julian called out.

Astrid's eyes shone. "She's everywhere now."

Julian nodded. "Her legacy shines brighter than any star."

Under Rachel's guidance, civilizations flourished. Planets once barren now teemed with life. The orb, now a celestial compass, directed explorers to hidden wonders.

Julian and Astrid roamed the galaxy, sharing Rachel's wisdom. Together, they forged a new era of peace and cooperation.

"Cosmic balance has been restored," Astrid said.

Julian smiled. "Rachel's spirit ignites the cosmos."

Rachel's symphony echoed through the galaxy. Stars sang in harmony, planets danced. Galactic balance was perfected.

Astrid smiled. "Rachel's legacy will endure forever."

Julian nodded. "Her spirit is eternal."

An ancient prophecy unfolded. "A cosmic guardian will rise."

Rachel's essence stirred. "A new threat emerges."

The galaxy responded, preparing for battle. Julian and Astrid stood ready.

"What's coming?" Julian asked.

Rachel's voice whispered. "The unknown."

Julian and Astrid patrolled the galaxy, ever vigilant.

Rachel's essence guided them, sensing disturbances.

A faint signal echoed from a distant planet.

"Anomaly detected," Astrid said.

Julian's eyes narrowed. "Let's investigate."

They landed on the planet, surrounded by ancient ruins.

Rachel's essence stirred, unlocking secrets.

"An ancient civilization," Astrid whispered.

Julian's gaze swept the horizon. "And a hidden threat."

A structure rose, emitting energy.

"What is this?" Julian asked.

Rachel's voice whispered. "A gateway."

Chapter 14: Gateway to the Unknown

The gateway activated, revealing a wormhole.
    Julian and Astrid exchanged a glance.
    "Rachel, what lies beyond?" Julian asked.
    Rachel's essence pulsed. "The unknown."
    Julian and Astrid stepped into the wormhole.
    Rachel's essence enveloped them, guiding their journey.
    Stars blurred, space-time distorted.
    They emerged in a realm beyond their galaxy.
    Ancient structures towered, emitting mystical energy.
    Julian's eyes widened. "This is impossible."
    Astrid's voice filled with awe. "Rachel's legacy."
    A figure approached, cloaked in shadows.
    "Welcome, guardians," the figure said.
    The figure revealed itself: an ancient being.
    "I hold secrets of the cosmos," it said.
    Rachel's essence stirred, curious.
    "What secrets?" Julian asked.
    The ancient being smiled. "The origin of the universe."

STARLIGHT ODYSSEY

Chapter 15: Cosmic Origins

The ancient being's words echoed through Julian's mind. "The origin of the universe?" he repeated, his voice barely above a whisper.

Astrid's eyes sparkled with curiosity. "Tell us," she urged.

The ancient being nodded, its presence shimmering with an otherworldly energy. "In the beginning, there was the Void," it began. "An endless expanse of nothingness, punctuated by a single point of light."

Rachel's essence pulsed, as if resonating with the ancient being's words.

"That point of light expanded, birthing the universe," the being continued. "Matter coalesced, forming galaxies and stars. Life emerged, evolving into complex forms."

Julian's mind reeled, struggling to comprehend the sheer scale of creation.

"What about the Quantum Core?" Astrid asked, her voice filled with determination.

The ancient being's smile grew wider. "Ah, the Quantum Core. A key to unlocking the universe's secrets, hidden within the fabric of space-time."

Rachel's essence stirred, as if urging Julian and Astrid onward.

"Come," the ancient being said. "Witness the birth of the universe."

The ancient being led Julian and Astrid through a shimmering portal. They found themselves floating amidst swirling clouds of gas and dust.

A brilliant light illuminated the cosmos. Stars burst forth, their radiance casting an ethereal glow.

Planets coalesced, their orbits weaving a celestial tapestry. Life sprouted, evolving from simple organisms to complex civilizations.

Rachel's essence resonated with the universe's symphony.

"This is incredible," Astrid whispered.

Julian's gaze swept the cosmic landscape. "We're witnessing the universe's birth."

The ancient being's voice whispered in their minds. "Remember, guardians. The Quantum Core holds the key to balancing the universe's energies."

Chapter 16: Balance of the Cosmos

As they returned to the ancient structure, Julian felt an overwhelming sense of purpose.

"What must we do?" Astrid asked, determination etched on her face.

Rachel's essence pulsed. "Restore balance to the Quantum Core."

The ancient being nodded. "The fate of the universe depends on it."

With newfound resolve, Julian and Astrid stepped forward, ready to face the challenges ahead.

Will they succeed in restoring balance to the Quantum Core?

Julian and Astrid stood before the ancient being, determination burning within them. "We won't fail," Julian vowed.

Astrid's eyes shone with conviction. "We'll restore balance to the Quantum Core."

The ancient being's smile held mystical depths. "The prophecy unfolds. Rachel's essence guides you."

Suddenly, visions flooded Julian's mind: swirling energies, quantum fluctuations and the Cosmic Horizon's secrets.

"The path ahead," the ancient being whispered, "is fraught with danger. Time and space converge."

Julian and Astrid stepped into the wormhole, Rachel's essence enveloping them. Stars blurred, space-time distorted.

They emerged near the NeuroSphere facility, now a hub of frantic activity.

Dr. Patel rushed toward them. "Julian, Astrid! We've stabilized the Quantum Core, but—"

"A temporal convergence is happening," Julian interrupted, visions still seared in his mind.

Astrid's grip on her weapon tightened. "We must protect the Core."

Forces converged on NeuroSphere: rival factions, ancient enemies and time-travelers.

Julian, Astrid and Dr. Patel's team defended the Quantum Core against those seeking to exploit its power.

Rachel's essence surged, amplifying Julian's abilities.

In the heart of the battle, an unexpected ally emerged.

As the battle raged on, Julian's thoughts drifted to his troubled past. His parents, renowned scientists, had disappeared during an experiment when he was a teenager. The incident left emotional scars.

Astrid's gaze met Julian's, her expression softening. "Hey, focus!" she shouted above the din.

Julian snapped back to reality, his determination renewed.

Astrid's Backstory

Astrid's thoughts wandered to her own past. Growing up on the streets, she had to rely on her wits and fists. Her natural talent for combat earned her a spot in an elite military unit.

But the memories of her fallen comrades continued to haunt her.

Dr. Patel's Secrets

Dr. Patel's eyes locked onto Julian, her expression a mix of concern and admiration. She recalled her own journey: a brilliant mind, driven by curiosity and a hidden agenda.

Her thoughts whispered: "The Quantum Core holds more than energy – it holds the key to unlocking humanity's true potential."

Rachel's Legacy

Rachel's essence pulsed, her presence woven into the fabric of the Quantum Core. Her memories unfolded: love, loss and sacrifice.

"Julian," Rachel's voice whispered in his mind, "balance the Core, restore hope."

Chapter 17: Hidden Motives

As forces clashed, tensions escalated. Alliances were tested.

Dr. Patel approached Julian. "We need to recalibrate the Quantum Core. Trust me."

Astrid hesitated. "What's your true agenda, Doctor?"

Dr. Patel's smile hinted at secrets untold. "The future of humanity hangs in balance."

Julian's instincts screamed caution, but Rachel's essence reassured him.

"Trust her," Rachel whispered.

Julian nodded, trusting Rachel's guidance. "Let's do it, Dr. Patel."

Astrid's eyes narrowed. "We're risking everything."

Dr. Patel's hands flew across the console. "We're altering the Quantum Core's resonance frequency."

The room hummed with tension as calculations streamed across screens.

The Quantum Core pulsed, its energy signature shifting.

Rachel's essence swirled, merging with the Core.

Astrid's grip on her weapon tightened. "What's happening?"

Dr. Patel's eyes sparkled. "Resonance achieved."

The Quantum Core's glow stabilized, its power now balanced.

Julian exhaled, relief washing over him.

Astrid's smile hinted at pride. "We did it."

Dr. Patel's expression turned contemplative. "This changes everything."

Chapter 18: New Horizons

The NeuroSphere facility transformed into a hub of discovery. Scientists flocked to unlock the Quantum Core's secrets. Julian, Astrid and Dr. Patel stood at the forefront.

Rachel's essence whispered, "The universe awaits."

A shimmering portal emerged from the Quantum Core.

Astrid's eyes widened. "A gateway to the cosmos."

Julian's heart raced. "Where does it lead?"

Dr. Patel's smile held wonder. "Let's find out."

Julian's hand reached out, hesitating before touching the shimmering portal. Astrid's gaze met his, excitement and trepidation mingling. Dr. Patel's voice filled the silence. "This gateway holds secrets of the universe. Let's uncover them."

With a deep breath, Julian stepped forward, Astrid beside him. The portal enveloped them, colors blurring as they traversed the vast expanse. Stars streaked past, like diamonds on velvet. Nebulae unfolded, ethereal curtains of gas and dust.

Chapter 19: Celestial Odyssey

They emerged on the edge of a nebula, its swirling clouds shimmering. Astrid's gasp echoed through the void. "Incredible." A celestial city floated within the nebula's heart, shimmering spires reaching toward the stars.

Julian's awe was palpable. "An ancient civilization." Dr. Patel's eyes sparkled. "One holding secrets of the cosmos."

The trio approached the city, guarded by beings of pure energy. Their forms shifted, like liquid light. "Welcome, travelers," one being said. "We have awaited you."

Rachel's essence stirred within Julian. "These guardians hold the universe's truths."

Within the city's heart, an ancient artifact pulsed. The guardians' leader spoke, "This artifact holds the universe's origins." Dr. Patel's hands reached out, reverence in her eyes.

As the artifact activated, visions flooded their minds: cosmic birth, celestial dance and the Quantum Core's secrets.

Chapter 20: Legacy Unveiled

The visions faded, leaving stunned silence. Astrid whispered, "The universe's secrets." Julian's gaze locked onto Dr. Patel. "What does this mean?"

Dr. Patel's smile was radiant. "We hold the key to unlocking humanity's potential."*Chapter

Dr. Patel's eyes shone with excitement. "The artifact revealed the universe's blueprint. We can harness this knowledge to elevate human consciousness."

Astrid leaned in, intrigued. "Explain, Doctor."

"The Quantum Core resonates with humanity's collective unconscious," Dr. Patel began. "By synchronizing our minds with its frequency, we can tap into limitless potential."

Julian's mind raced. "Telepathy, telekinesis?"

Dr. Patel nodded. "And more. Enhanced cognition, accelerated healing. Humanity's next evolution."

Chapter 21: The Quantum Leap

Rachel's essence pulsed, resonating with Dr. Patel's words.

"The Quantum Core's balance restored, we can initiate the quantum leap," Dr. Patel announced.

Astrid's determination hardened. "Let's do this."

Julian's resolve deepened. "Together, we'll unlock humanity's future."

NeuroSphere's team worked tirelessly, constructing a global network.

Dr. Patel oversaw the operation. "When activated, this network will synchronize human consciousness with the Quantum Core."

Astrid and Julian stood ready, their bond stronger than ever.

The network hummed to life. Energy surged, enveloping the planet.

Humanity's collective unconscious stirred, awakening dormant potential.

*As the energy dissipated, silence fell.

The first thought echoed through minds worldwide:

"We are one."

Dedication

I'd like to dedicate this book to my family and friends.

A Cosmic Horizon Started out as a personal project on TikTok just something fun to past time. As it grew into what you're about to read I met some really awesome people along the way I'm just gonna give usernames.

A dear friend of mine, A Fellow author under the pseudonym Sam LaRose gave me a lot of inspiration and motivation. Sometimes I wanted to give up and she encouraged me to keep going. Thank you for that Sam.

A bright star in this universe under the username Sunshyne Smilez, which I took inspiration to add her as a character because of her kind spirit and loving heart. Thank you for always being a good friend and motivating me to think outside of myself.

A dear friend of mine once told me, "Before you commit to anything, you need to ask yourself why you're having any reservations and be honest with yourself about it...don't look back and regret something and make sure you're going into it fully aware that things might not happen exactly the way you think they might and I know I don't even probably have to say that to you but I do because if I didn't say it, I'd feel like $@!/ lol but that's not to say I have a bad feeling about this cause I don't." Words of wisdom from BG.

You're right BG I thank you for always being a voice of reason.

As a lot of us know, life can be busy and you don't get to see your family members as often as you would like. As I wrote this book I did spend a lot of time on TikTok with my family online, but I also got to enjoy brief moments with my sister Jennifer my cousin Christina, Charlie, David, Crystal of course my nieces and nephew and I spend time with my parents

I'd like to think each one of y'all for listening to me ramble on about some far away universe called TikTok, but in reality not so much reality it was the making of A Cosmic Horizon I appreciate you, letting me bend your ear

I'd like to take one more moment of your time to remember the loved ones that were lost during the journey Sissy Tammy, and Grandpa Fontenot, and my stepmom Linda I know y'all all would've been proud of me miss y'all every day

And thank you to all my readers. I really do appreciate you I Hope you enjoy the book.

Part One: A Cosmic Horizon

A cosmic Horizon

Chapter 1: Dr. Patel

In the year 2154, humanity had reached the pinnacle of technological advancement. Scientists at the prestigious research facility, NeuroSphere, had discovered a way to harness the power of quantum energy. Led by the brilliant and charismatic Dr. Sofia Patel, the team had created a device capable of tapping into the infinite potential of the quantum realm.

The device, known as the Quantum Core, glowed with an ethereal blue light as it hummed to life. As the team watched in awe, the Quantum Core began to generate an immense amount of energy. It was as if the very fabric of space and time was being unlocked, revealing a hidden reservoir of power. The implications were profound. With quantum energy, humanity could solve the world's energy crisis, explore the depths of space, and unlock new technologies previously thought impossible.

But as the team delved deeper into the mysteries of the Quantum Core, they began to realize the true magnitude of their discovery. The device was not only generating energy, but also creating a rift in the quantum field, threatening to unravel the very fabric of reality. Dr. Patel and her team raced against time to understand and control the Quantum Core's power. They knew that if they failed, the consequences would be catastrophic. The fate of humanity hung in the balance, as the team struggled to harness the infinite potential of quantum energy.

Would they succeed, or would the Quantum Core's power consume them all?

The world held its breath as the scientists at Neuro Sphere pushed the boundaries of human knowledge, venturing into theunknown. As the team worked tirelessly to understand and control the Quantum Core, they began to experience strange occurrences. Equipment would malfunction, and strange noises echoed through the facility. Some team members even reported seeing glimpses of alternate realities.

Chapter 2: Quantum Core

Dr. Patel realized that the Quantum Core was not only generating energy but also creating a rift in the fabric of space-time. The team was torn between the thrill of discovery and the terror of the unknown.

One fateful night, the Quantum Core surged to critical levels. The team scrambled to shut it down, but it was too late. A blinding flash of light filled the room, and the fabric of reality tore apart. The team found themselves hurtled through alternate dimensions, witnessing realities beyond their wildest dreams. They saw worlds where humanity had never existed, and others where technology had consumed all.

Dr. Patel realized that the Quantum Core had become a gateway to the multiverse. The team had unlocked the secrets of the cosmos, but at what cost?

As they navigated the vast expanse of the multiverse, the team encountered strange creatures and alternate versions of themselves. They began to question their own reality and the true nature of existence. Would they find a way back to their own reality, or would they be forever lost in the infinite possibilities of the multiverse?

The journey through the Quantum Core had begun, and the fate of humanity hung in the balance. As they traversed the multiverse, the team encountered a reality where humanity had made contact with intelligent extraterrestrial life. They witnessed a world where technology had merged with biology, creating a new form of sentient life.

Dr. Patel's team discovered a reality where the laws of physics were reversed, and gravity pulled objects away from each other instead of attracting them. They saw a universe where time flowed backwards, and the fabric of reality was unraveling. The team's minds reeled as they struggled to comprehend the infinite possibilities of the multiverse. They began to question their own sanity and the nature of reality.

Suddenly, they stumbled upon a reality that was identical to their own, except for one stark difference - the Quantum Core had never been built. The team realized that they had the power to alter the course of history and change the fate of humanity. Would they use this knowledge to shape the destiny of their own reality, or would they continue to explore the infinite possibilities of the multiverse? The journey through the Quantum Core had become a journey of self-discovery, as the team grappled with the weight of their newfound power.

Chapter 3: The Cosmic Calling

Maya stood at the edge of the spacecraft, gazing out at the curved horizon of Earth. She felt a mix of emotions: excitement for the journey ahead, and a hint of sadness at leaving her home planet behind. The thrill of adventure had always called to her, and now she was finally answering.

As a renowned astrophysicist, Maya had spent years studying the mysteries of the universe. She had devoted herself to unlocking the secrets of space and time, and her work had led to groundbreaking discoveries. But despite her many accomplishments, she couldn't shake the feeling that there was still so much more to explore.

The spacecraft's engines roared to life, and Maya felt a rumble beneath her feet. She took a deep breath, savoring the moment. This was it - the start of her greatest adventure yet. With a final farewell to Earth, Maya embarked on a journey through the cosmos. She was bound for the unknown, driven by a sense of wonder and a thirst for knowledge.

Little did she know, her travels would soon lead her to a remarkable encounter - one that would change the course of her life forever. The stars ahead beckoned, and Maya's heart soared with excitement. She was leaving Earth behind, but the universe was full of secrets waiting to be uncovered. And she was ready to explore them all.

Chapter 4: The Cosmic Companion

Maya's journey through the universe was filled with wonder and discovery. She traveled to new worlds, met new civilizations, and uncovered secrets of the cosmos. But despite the thrill of exploration, she couldn't shake the feeling of loneliness. She longed for a companion to share her adventures with.

One day, as she was exploring a particularly vibrant planet, she stumbled upon a being unlike any she had ever seen.

It was a small, radiant creature with wings like a butterfly and hair like a sunbeam.

Its name was Sunshine, and it was a being of pure joy and light. Sunshine was drawn to Maya's adventurous spirit and her desire to explore the universe. It attached itself to her, becoming her constant companion and friend.

Together, they traveled the cosmos, discovering new wonders and facing new challenges. With Sunshine by her side, Maya felt a sense of belonging she had never known before. She no longer felt alone in the vast expanse of space. Sunshine's presence filled her with warmth and happiness, and she knew that she could face anything the universe threw their way.

As they journeyed, Sunshine proved to be more than just a loyal companion. It possessed a deep understanding of the universe and its workings. It could sense the vibrations of the cosmos, and it often warned Maya of impending dangers. Maya was grateful for Sunshine's guidance and protection. She realized that she had been given a rare gift - a friend who was not only a companion but also a guardian and a mentor.

Together, Maya and Sunshine explored the unknown reaches of the universe, uncovering secrets and marvels beyond their wildest dreams. And as they traveled, they knew that their bond would last a lifetime, a shining beacon of hope and friendship in the vast expanse of space.

Chapter 5: The Quantum Connection

Maya and Sunshine's adventures took them to the farthest reaches of the universe, where they encountered strange and mysterious phenomena. One day, while exploring a distant galaxy, they stumbled upon a peculiar object - a small, glowing orb that seemed to defy the laws of physics.

As they approached the orb, they felt a strange energy emanating from it, like a vibration that resonated deep within their souls. Without warning, the orb began to glow brighter, and Maya and Sunshine found themselves being pulled into a quantum realm.

In this realm, the laws of physics no longer applied. Time and space were fluid, and the very fabric of reality was twisted and distorted. Maya and Sunshine found themselves hurtling through a wormhole, their minds reeling from the sheer strangeness of it all.

As they emerged from the wormhole, they found themselves in a realm unlike any they had ever seen. The sky was a deep purple, and the ground was covered in a thick, iridescent mist. Strange creatures flitted about, their forms shifting and morphing as they moved. Maya and Sunshine knew they had to find a way back to their own universe, but the quantum realm was full of dangers. They had to navigate its treacherous landscapes and avoid the creatures that lurked within.

As they journeyed through the realm, they encountered a being unlike any they had ever met. It was a quantum entity, a being of pure energy that existed beyond the bounds of space and time. The entity spoke to them in a language that was both familiar and yet completely alien.

"You have entered this realm for a reason," it said. "You have a role to play in the balance of the universe."

Maya and Sunshine were intrigued. They knew that their adventures had a purpose, but they had never imagined that they would be drawn into a quantum realm.

"What is our role?" Maya asked, her mind racing with possibilities.

"You will know when the time comes," the entity replied.

"For now, you must navigate the dangers of this realm and find your way back to your own universe."

And with that, the entity vanished, leaving Maya and Sunshine to face the challenges of the quantum realm alone.

Chapter 6: The Voice of Sunshine

Maya and Sunshine continued their journey through the quantum realm, facing strange and wondrous challenges at every turn. As they navigated the treacherous landscapes, Sunshine began to speak to Maya in a voice that was both gentle and powerful.

"Maya, I have a purpose," Sunshine said, its voice like a warm breeze on a summer day. "I am not just a companion, but a guide. I have been sent to help you unlock the secrets of the universe."

Maya was amazed. She had never heard Sunshine speak before, and she didn't know that it had a purpose beyond being a loyal friend.

"What secrets?" Maya asked, her curiosity piqued.

"The secrets of the cosmos," Sunshine replied. "The secrets of life and death, of space and time. You have been chosen to unlock these secrets, Maya. And I am here to guide you on your journey."

Maya was stunned. She had never imagined that her adventures with Sunshine would lead to something so profound.

As they journeyed deeper into the quantum realm, Sunshine began to reveal its purpose in more detail. It was a being of pure energy, created by the universe itself to guide Maya on her quest for knowledge. With Sunshine by her side, Maya felt a sense of purpose and meaning that she had never known before. She knew that she was not just exploring the universe for its own sake, but for a greater purpose - to unlock the secrets of the cosmos and bring light to the darkness.

Together, Maya and Sunshine faced the challenges of the quantum realm, using their combined strength and wisdom to overcome the obstacles in their path. And as they journeyed on, they knew that their bond would last a lifetime, a shining beacon of hope and friendship in the vast expanse of space.

Chapter 7: Day-to-Day Life in the Quantum Realm

Maya and Sunshine's journey through the quantum realm was not without its challenges, but they had grown accustomed to the strange and wondrous landscapes that surrounded them. As they traveled, they began to settle into a day-to-day routine, finding moments of beauty and joy in the midst of their adventures.

Each morning, Maya would wake up in their makeshift camp, surrounded by the glowing mist of the quantum realm. She would stretch her arms and legs, feeling the strange energy of the realm coursing through her veins. Sunshine would be by her side, its radiant form glowing softly in the dim light. After a quick breakfast, they would set off into the unknown, exploring the ever-changing landscapes of the realm.

They would walk for hours, taking in the sights and sounds of the strange world around them. Maya would ask Sunshine questions about the realm and its secrets, and Sunshine would answer in its gentle, wisdom-filled voice. As the day wore on, they would come across strange creatures and obstacles, which they would overcome using their combined strength and ingenuity. Maya would use her knowledge of the universe to navigate the challenges, while Sunshine would offer guidance and support whenever needed.

In the evenings, they would return to their camp, exhausted but exhilarated by their adventures. Maya would sit by a glowing fire, watching the stars twinkle to life in the sky above. Sunshine would sit beside her, its form glowing softly in the flickering light. As they sat in silence, Maya would feel a deep sense of connection to the universe and its secrets. She knew that she and Sunshine were on a journey of discovery, uncovering the hidden truths of the cosmos. And she knew that their bond would last a lifetime, a shining beacon of hope and friendship in the vast expanse of space.

Chapter 8: A New Beginning

Maya and Sunshine's adventures through the quantum realm had come to an end, but their journey together was far from over. As they stood before a shimmering portal, Maya knew that it was time to return to her own universe, but she was grateful that Sunshine would be by her side.

"Thank you for everything, Sunshine," Maya said, her voice filled with emotion. "You've been my guide, my friend, and my shining star. I couldn't have done it without you."

Sunshine's form glowed brightly, and it spoke in a voice that was both gentle and powerful.

"We're not done yet, Maya. We have a whole new universe to explore together. And I'll always be here to guide you, to support you, and to smile with you."

With that, Maya and Sunshine stepped through the portal.

Chapter 9: Time has past for Maya and Jack

As they rested, Maya's eyes widened suddenly, her gaze fixed on a distant vision.

"What is it, Maya?" Jack asked, concern etched on his face.

"I saw something," Maya replied, her voice barely above a whisper. "A vision from

Sunshine. Dr. Patel... she used the Quantum Core to travel through the multiverse."

Jack's eyes widened in awe. "Whoa, that's heavy. A whole different level of sci-fi stuff!"

Sunshine's radiant form materialized before them, its light pulsing with an otherworldly energy.

"I can take you to Earth, to a parallel timeline where humans may be able to aid you in your fight against Zorvath," Sunshine offered, its voice like a gentle breeze.

Maya's eyes locked onto Sunshine, searching for any sign of deception. But Sunshine's form pulsed with an reassuring light, its presence emanating warmth and trustworthiness.

"Can we trust you?" Maya asked, her voice still laced with uncertainty.

Sunshine's form glowed brighter, its light enveloping Maya and Jack. "I am bound to help you, Maya. I have watched over you since the beginning. We must act quickly, before Zorvath'sfleet arrives. The fate of the multiverse depends on it."

Maya's eyes met Jack's, and they shared a nod of determination.

"Alright, let's do it," Jack said, his voice firm.

Chapter 10: Times Square

With Sunshine guiding them, they embarked on a journey through the Quantum Core Sunshine opened, hurtling them through wormholes and alternate realities and throwing them into what once was Times Square, once a vibrant and bustling hub of entertainment, now lay in ruins. The streets were desolate and eerily silent, littered with debris and the remnants of what once was. The iconic billboards and neon lights that once illuminated the night sky now hung dimly, flickering with a faint, otherworldly glow.

Maya gazed out at the desolate landscape of Times Square, her eyes scanning the ruins. She turned to Jack with a wry smile and said, "Well, I guess this is what they mean by 'The Great White Way' now. More like the Great White Elephant, am I right?"

Jack chuckled, shaking his head. "Only you, Maya, can find humor in the apocalypse."

Maya shrugged, her smile fading. "Hey, someone's got to keep things interesting around here. Otherwise, we'd just be wandering around in silence, waiting for the end to come."

Jack nodded, his expression serious. "You're right. We need to keep our spirits up, no matter what. And if wit and sarcasm are what get us through this, then so be it."

Maya grinned, her eyes sparkling with mischief. "That's the spirit, Jack. Now, shall we get moving? I hear the ruins of the Empire State Building are lovely this time of year."

As they navigated the treacherous landscape, Maya's quick wit and sharp tongue continued to slice through the tension. Jack found himself laughing despite the dire circumstances, grateful for her presence.

"Hey, Maya?" Jack said, ducking beneath a fallen beam.

"Yeah?" she replied, her eyes scanning the horizon.

"If we make it out of this alive, I'm buying you a drink. Or ten."

Maya's grin flashed in the dim light. "Deal! But only if you promise to listen to me complain about the apocalypse for hours on end."

Jack chuckled, shaking his head. "I wouldn't have it any other way."

As they pressed on, the ruins of the city gave way to a eerie silence. The only sound was the soft crunch of gravel beneath their feet, a haunting reminder of the desolation that surrounded them.

Suddenly, Maya's head snapped up, her eyes fixed on something in the distance.

"Jack, look."

He followed her gaze, his heart sinking as he saw it: a plume of smoke rising from the heart of the city, a beacon of danger in an already treacherous world.

"What do you think it is?" Maya asked, her voice barely above a whisper. Jack's expression was grim. "Only one way to find out."With a deep breath, they set off towards the smoke, ready to face whatever lay ahead.

As they approached the source of the smoke, they saw a figure huddled beside a makeshift lab, surrounded by debris and twisted metal. The figure slowly stood, revealing a woman with a determined look on her face.

"Dr. Patel!" Jack exclaimed, surprise etched on his face.

"Jack! Maya!" Dr. Patel replied, her eyes filled with a mix of relief and urgency. "I'm so glad you're here. I've been working on a way to stabilize the cosmic portal."

Maya's eyes widened. "You mean the one that brought us here?"

Dr. Patel nodded. " Yes. I created it, hoping to bridge the gap between parallel universes. But it's been malfunctioning, causing chaos in both worlds."

Jack's expression turned serious. "We've seen the destruction firsthand. Can you fix it?"

Dr. Patel hesitated. "I've been trying, but I need your help. The portal's energy signature is tied to your presence here. I need you to reactivate it, so I can realign the frequencies."

Maya's eyes met Jack's, then returned to Dr. Patel.

"What's the catch?"

Dr. Patel's face was grim.

"The process could be dangerous. We'll need to be quick, before Zorvath's fleet detects our presence."

Jack nodded.

"Let's do it. We can't leave this world in ruins."

Dr. Patel led them to the portal, her hands moving swiftly across the console.

"Ready?"

Maya took a deep breath.

"Ready."

Jack nodded.

"Let's end this."

With a burst of energy, the portal roared to life, its colors swirling wildly. Dr. Patel worked feverishly; her eyes fixed on the readouts.

The machine hummed, building in intensity.

Dr. Patel's eyes locked onto the console, her fingers flying across the controls.

"Energy levels are stabilizing! We need to act fast, before Zorvath's fleet detects our presence!"

Jack's mind raced.

"We need an army to take on forces in the alternate universe."

Maya's eyes widened. "But where can we find one?"

Dr. Patel's gaze met theirs. "I've been working on a plan. We can recruit allies from various timelines, using the portal to bring them here."

Jack's eyes lit up.

"You mean, like a multiverse coalition?"

Dr. Patel nodded. "Exactly! With the portal's power, we can gather a formidable force to take on Zorvath's army."

With her device, she had gathered a vast array of weapons, technologies, and strategic information from various dimensions. She had also formed alliances with powerful beings from other worlds, who had pledged their support in the battle against Zorvath.

As she worked, Jack and Maya stood guard, protecting her from any potential threats.

They had seen the devastation that Zorvath's army was capable of, and they knew that Dr. Patel's work was crucial to their survival. With each new discovery,

Dr. Patel's determination grew. She was convinced that with the right resources and knowledge, they could defeat Zorvath and restore peace to their worlds.

Finally, after weeks of tireless work, Dr. Patel had gathered everything they needed. She stood up, her eyes shining with determination.

"It's time," she said. "We have everything we need to take down Zorvath's army."

Jack and Maya nodded, They gathered allies and knowledge, piecing together a plan to defeat Zorvath's fleet. Their new allies joined forces with them, sharing knowledge and strategies. Together, they prepared for the ultimate showdown against Zorvath's fleet.

"Thank you," Maya said, her voice filled with gratitude. "We couldn't have done it without you Sunshine."

Sunshine's form pulsed with a warm light, its presence a reminder of the trust they had placed in each other. "We make a good team, Maya. Together, we can face anything the multiverse throws our way."

Maya's determination grew.

"Let's do it! We can't let Zorvath destroy entire universes."

Part Two: A Cosmic Reckoning

Chapter 11: The Zorvath's Rise to Power

The stars had gone dark, and the last remnants of humanity were held captive by an alien race known as the Zorvath. These towering, slender beings had conquered Earth with ease, and now used humans as test subjects for their twisted scientific experiments.

Astronaut Jack Harris found himself among the prisoners, forced to toil in the Zorvath's underground labs. But Jack refused to give up, and soon discovered that the aliens' technology was not infallible. He formed a secret alliance with a small group of humans, and together they began to sabotage the Zorvath'sequipment and gather intel on their captors. As they dug deeper, Jack and his team uncovered a shocking truth: the Zorvath were not just conquerors, but also survivors.

Their own planet had been destroyed in a catastrophic event, and they sought to harness humanity's biological diversity to revive their own dying species. With this knowledge, Jack and the humans hatched a daring plan to overthrow their alien overlords and reclaim their place in the universe. But the Zorvath would not go quietly into the night...

The rebellion began with a series of subtle sabotage acts, targeting the Zorvath's vital equipment and disrupting their experiments. But as the humans' confidence grew, so did their boldness. They launched a full-scale assault on the alien stronghold, fighting their way through the Zorvath's towering warriors and deadly drones.

Jack led the charge, his determination fueled by the memory of his lost loved ones and the hope of a free future. The battle raged on, with both sides suffering heavy losses. Just as the humans seemed to gain the upper hand, the Zorvath's ruthless leader, the Overlord Xarath, unleashed a devastating weapon: a mindcontrol device that turned the humans' own allies against them.

Jack found himself facing off against his own comrades, their eyes blank and their actions controlled by the Zorvath's sinister technology. With a heavy heart, he fought his way through the brainwashed humans, determined to reach Xarath and shatter the mind-control device.

In a final, brutal confrontation, Jack faced the Overlord Xarath. The two enemies clashed in a fierce hand-to-hand combat, their strength and cunning evenly matched. But Jack's human spirit proved stronger, and he managed to destroy the mind-control device, treeing his comrades from the Zorvath's grasp.

With the aliens' hold broken, the humans reclaimed their planet, and Jack became a hero to his people. But as they began to rebuild, they knew that the universe was full of secrets and dangers, and that their struggle for survival was far from over...

As the dust settled, a young and charismatic leader emerged among the humans: Maya Blackwood, a former scientist who had lost her family to the Zorvath's experiments. With her quick wit, strategic mind, and tierce determination, Maya rallied the humans and helped them rebuild their shattered world. Under Maya's leadership, the humans formed a new government, the Earth Resistance, and began to reclaim their planet from the Zorvath'sruins. They scavenged technology, formed alliances, and trained a new generation of warriors to defend their home world.

But the Zorvath, though defeated, were far from vanquished. Xarath's successor, the cunning and ruthless Overlord Lyra, vowed to crush the human uprising and restore her people's dominance. Lyra launched a series of guerrilla attacks, using the Zorvath'sadvanced technology to strike at the humans' weak points. Maya, anticipating Lyra's tactics, developed a counter-strategy. She formed an elite team of humans, each with unique skills and expertise, to infiltrate the Zorvath's ranks and gather crucial intel. Among them was Jack Harris, the astronaut who had sparked the rebellion, now a seasoned warrior and Maya's trusted ally.

Together, Maya and Jack led the humans in a perilous game of cat and mouse, outmaneuvering the Zorvath at every turn. But Lyra had a secret weapon: a powerful, ancient artifact hidden deep within the Zorvath's stronghold, capable of bending the fabric of space and time...

Chapter 12: Lyra unleashed the artifact's

Lyra unleashed the artifact's power, creating a rift in space-time that allowed the Zorvath to launch a devastating attack on the human resistance. Maya and Jack's team fought valiantly, but they were vastly outnumbered and outgunned. The Zorvathoverwhelmed them, capturing key strongholds and pushing the humans to the brink of defeat.

In a last-ditch effort, Maya and Jack led a small group of rebels in a desperate bid to destroy the artifact and shatter the Zorvath's hold on the planet. They infiltrated the Zorvath'sstronghold, avoiding deadly traps and battling elite warriors to reach the heart of the fortress.

But Lyra was waiting for them, her eyes blazing with triumph. With a flick of her wrist, she activated the artifact, unleashing a blast of energy that sent Maya and Jack flying across the room.

As they struggled to get back to their feet, Lyra revealed her ultimate plan: to use the artifact to merge the Zorvath's dimension with Earth's, enslaving humanity forever.

With a cackle, Lyra activated the artifact, and the room began to distort and blur. Maya and Jack knew they had to act fast - but how could they defeat an enemy with the power of a god?

In a flash of inspiration, Jack remembered an ancient human technology that might counter the artifact's energy. He and Maya raced against time to reactivate the device, dodging Lyra's deadly attacks and t' Zorvath's relentless warriors.

Just as the artifact was about to merge the dimensions, Jack and Maya activated the counter-device, unleashing a burst of energy that disrupted the artifact's power. The rift in space-time began to close, and the Zorvath's hold on Earth began to falter.

Enraged, Lya altacked Maya and Jack with her bare hands, but the two rebels fought back with every ounce of strength they had. In a final, brutal blow, Maya struck Lyra down, shattering the Zorvath's last hope for dominance.

As the dust settled, Maya and Jack stood victorious, but scarred by the battle. They knew that the war was far from over - but for now, they had saved humanity from the brink of destruction. The Zorvath's grip on Earth was broken, and the humans could finally begin to rebuild their shattered world.

Maya and Jack's victory over the Zorvath had brought a measure of peace to Earth, but the scars of the war still lingered. The humans had rebuilt their cities and their lives, but the memory of the Zorvath's brutality remained fresh in their minds.

Rumors began to circulate of a possible second attack, whispers of a new Zorvath fleet gathering in the depths of space. Maya, now the leader of the Earth Detense Force, took these rumors seriously, knowing that the Zorvath would not forgive their defeat so easily.

She and Jack, now her trusted advisor, worked tirelessly to strengthen Earth's defenses, developing new technologies and training a new generation of warriors. But despite their efforts, the humans were still vulnerable, and the Zorvath's return seemed inevitable.

One night, a strange energy signature appeared on the edge of the solar system. Maya and Jack knew immediately that this was no drill - the Zorvath were back, and they were not alone.

A new, even more powerful fleet had arrived, led by a mysterious and ruthless Zorvath warlord named Krael.

His ships were bigger, his weapons more deadly, and his warriors more numerous than ever before.

Maya and Jack knew that the humans could not face this new threat alone.

They needed allies, and fast. They turned to the other intelligent species of the galaxy, the ones who had watched the humans' struggle against the Zorvath with interest.

The humans formed a fragile alliance with the insectoid K'tk'tk and the enigmatic energy beings known as the Aetherians. Together, they prepared to face the Zorvath's second invasion, knowing that the fate of Earth and the galaxy hung in the balance.

As the Zorvath fleet approached, Maya and Jack stood ready, their hearts heavy with the weight of their responsibility. They knew that this war would be different, that the stakes were higher and the enemy more formidable than ever before.

But they also knew that the humans had something that the Zorvath did not— hope, determination, and the will to tight for their freedom, no matter the cost.

The battle against the Zorvath's second invasion was fierce and long, but the humans and their allies fought with all their might. Maya and Jack led the charge, using every trick in the book to outmaneuver the Zorvath's superior numbers.

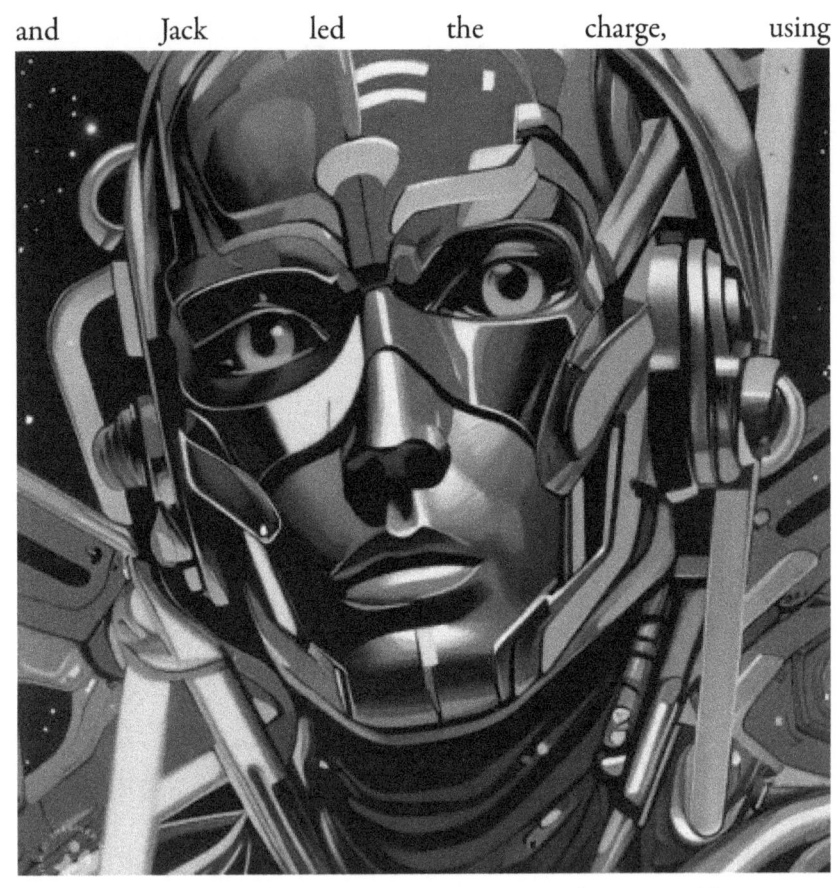

Just when it seemed like the tide was turning in favor of the humans, Krael unleashed his ultimate weapon: a massive energy cannon that could destroy entire planets. But the Aetherians, with their advanced technology, managed to neutralize the cannon, giving the humans a chance to counterattack.

With a final, decisive blow, the humans and their allies destroyed the Zorvath's fleet and shattered their hold on the galaxy. Krael was defeated and brought to justice and the Ovatireign of terror was finally over.

With the war won, the humans and their allies celebrated their hard-won victory. Maya and Jack were hailed as heroes, and their names became synonymous with bravery and leadership.

The humans, free from the Zorvath's tyranny, began to rebuild and explore the galaxy, making new friends and discovering new wonders.

The K'k't and Aetherians became valued allies, and together they formed a galactic community based on peace, cooperation, and mutual respect. Maya and Jack, now legendary figures, continued to serve as leaders and diplomats, helping to maintain the fragile balance of power in the galaxy.

They knew that there would always be challenges ahead, but they were confident that the humans and their allies were ready to face them together.

And so, the humans lived happily ever after, their future bright and full of promise, their hearts filled with hope and their spirits soaring with the knowledge that they had truly earned their place among the stars.

Chapter 13: The Zorvath's Rise to Power

In the distant reaches of the galaxy, a young and ambitious Zorvath named Xarath gazed out at the stars, dreaming of conquest and domination. His people, the Zorvath, were a nomadic and warlike species, always seeking new worlds to plunder and enslave.

Xarath, however, had a vision of something greater.

He saw a future where the Zorvath were not just raiders, but rulers - a future where they controlled the galaxy, and all other species bowed to their might. To achieve this dream, Xarath knew he needed power, and he was willing to do whatever it took to get it. He began to gather a loyal following of like-minded Zorvath, and together they set out to conquer and unite the warring factions of their people.

Their first target was the rival Zorvath clan, the Kraelions, who had long been a thorn in Xarath's side.

With cuning and ruthless tactics, Xarath and his followers defeated the Kraelions and absorbed their strength, growing their own power and influence.

As Xarath's reputation grew, so did his ambition. He set his sights on the nearby planet of K'tk'tk, home to a peaceful and advanced insectoid species. The Kttk were known for their wisdom and knowledge, and Xarath believed that with their secrets, he could conquer the entire galaxy...

Chapter 14: The Conquest of K'tk'tk

Xarath's plan to conquer K'tk'tk was met with skepticism by some of his followers.

"The K'tk't are a peaceful species," they argued.

"They will not pose a threat to us."

But Xarath knew better. He had studied the K'tk'tk, and he knew that their wisdom and knowledge made them a formidable foe.

He also knew that their advanced technology and strategic location in the galaxy made them a valuable prize.

Xarath's forces descended upon K'tk'tk like a swarm of locusts. The K'tk'tk, taken by surprise, put up a valiant resistance, but they were no match for the Zorvath's superior numbers and firepower.

As the K'tk'tk cities fell, Xarath's forces rounded up the survivors and brought them before their leader. The K'tk'tk queen, a wise and aged insectoid, gazed at Xarath with a mixture of sorrow and contempt.

"Why have you done this, Xarath?" she asked. "We meant you no harm."

Xarath sneered. "You are weak," he said.

"And the weak will always be conquered by the strong."

The K'tk'tk queen sighed.

"You will never be able to hold what you have taken," she said.

"The galaxy will rise up against you, and you will be cast down."

Xarath laughed.

" Will show you the true meaning of power,"
He said. And with that, he ordered his forces to enslave the K'tk'tk and plunder their planet.

The conquest of K'tk'tk was a turning point for Xarath and the Zorvath. It marked the beginning of their rise to dominance in the galaxy, and it set the stage for the conflicts that would follow.

The Rise of the Zorvath Empire

With the conquest of K'tk'tk, Xarath's power and influence grew exponentially. He declared himself Emperor of the Zorvath, and his followers hailed him as a hero.

Xarath's next target was the nearby planet of Aethoria, home to a ancient and mystical species known as the Aetherians. The Aetherians were known for their advanced technology and their deep understanding of the universe.

Chapter 15 :Overwhelmed

Xarath believed that with the Aetherians' secrets, he could unlock the secrets of the galaxy and cement the Zorvath's place as the dominant species. He launched a surprise attack on Aethoria, and the Aetherians, taken by surprise, were quickly overwhelmed.

The Aetherians' leader, the wise and enigmatic AetherianQueen Lyra, was brought before Xarath.

She gazed at him with a mixture of sadness and resignation.

"You have made a grave mistake, Xarath," she said.

"The Aetherians will not be enslaved. We will find a way to defeat you, and we will restore balance to the galaxy."

Xarath sneered.

"You are no match for the Zorvath," he said.

"We will crush all who oppose us."

And with that, he ordered his forces to enslave the Aetheriansand plunder their planet.

The Aetherians were forced to work in brutal conditions, building massive ships and weapons for the Zorvath.

The conquest of Aethoria marked the beginning of the Zorvath Empire's rapid expansion. Planet after planet fell to the Zorvath's might, and Xarath's power grew with each victory.

But the seeds of rebellion were already being sown.

The enslaved species were secretly planning their resistance, and the Zorvath's brutal tactics were fueling the fires of rebellion...

Chapter 16: The Rebellion Begins

As the Zorvath Empire continued its expansion, the enslaved species began to organize their resistance.

The K'tk'tk, Aetherians, and others formed a secret alliance, determined to overthrow the Zorvath and reclaim their freedom.

Their leader was a young human named Maya, who had lost her family to the Zorvath's brutality.

She was determined to bring down the empire and restore peace to the galaxy.

Maya and her allies launched a series of daring raids against the Zorvath, targeting their key installations and disrupting their supply lines. The Zorvath, taken by surprise, struggled to respond to the sudden uprising. Xarath, enraged by the rebellion, ordered his forces to crush the insurgents with brutal force. But the rebels would not be easily defeated.

As the war raged on, the rebels gained strength and support from other species who had suffered under the Zorvath's rule.

The tide of the conflict began to turn in their favor.

In a final, desperate bid to turn the tide, Xarath activated the ancient artifact he had discovered on Aethoria. The same artifact that had given him his power and ambition.

But the artifact had a secret. it was not just fool of conquest, but a key to unlocking the secrets of the universe.

And Maya, with her human intuition and compassion, was the only one who could wield its true power.

With the artifact's power coursing through her, Maya led the rebels in a final, decisive battle against the Zorvath. Xarath was defeated, and the empire was toppled.

The galaxy was finally free from the Zorvath's tyranny, and a new era of peace and cooperation began.

Maya, hailed as a hero, became the leader of a new galactic government, dedicated to protecting the freedom and dignity of all species.

And so, the story comes tull circle - from the rise of the Zorvath Empire to its downfall, and the dawn of a new era of peace and cooperation in the galaxy.

Chapter 17: A New Dawn

With the Zorvath Empire defeated and the galaxy finally at peace, humanity began to flourish.

Maya, now the leader of the galactic government, worked tirelessly to promote cooperation and understanding among the various species.

On Earth, human activity began to shift from survival mode to exploration and discovery.

Scientists and explorers ventured out into the galaxy, seeking new worlds and new civilizations to learn from and befriend.

As the days passed, humans began to notice something strange. The daylight hours seemed to be growing longer, and the nights shorter. At first, they thought it was just a trick of the light, but as the phenomenon continued, they realized that something was amiss.

Maya called upon the greatest minds in the galaxy to investigate the strange occurrence. After weeks of research, they discovered that the artifact, still resonating with power, was affecting the fabric of space-time itself.

The artifact it seemed, was not just a tool of conquest, but a key to unlocking the secrets of the universe.

And Maya, with her human intuition and compassion, had unwittingly triggered a new era of enlightenment and understanding.

As the days grew longer and brighter, humans and other species began to experience a new sense of unity and purpose.

They realized that they were not alone in the universe, and that their actions had consequences beyond their own world.

And so, with the artifact's power guiding them, humanity and the galaxy entered a new era of peace, cooperation, and discovery.

The daylight hours continued to grow, symbolizing the bright future that lay ahead. together, ready to face whatever adventures lay ahead.

As they emerged on the other side, Maya found herself back on Earth, surrounded by the beauty of the natural world.

But she knew that she would never be alone, for Sunshine was by her side, its radiant form shining brightly in the sunlight.

Epilogue

Maya and Sunshine lived out their days on Earth, exploring the wonders of the natural world, and sharing their knowledge and wisdom with all who would listen.

As they walked together under the stars, Sunshine's smile shone brightly, a beacon of hope and joy in the universe.
Coming Soon: Event Horizon of Forever
BOUND FOR THE UNKNOWN!
WHAT GREAT ADVENTURES LAY AHEAD FOR MAYA AND JACK AS THEY EMERGE ON THE OTHER SIDE, OF THE UNIVERSE WITH MORE EXCITEMENT ON THE WAY!
Chapter 1: Jack and Maya The Celestial Encounter....
Jack navigated his ship, the Starblade, through the Orion Nebula. Suddenly, a strange energy signature appeared on his radar. As he investigated, a stunning spacecraft emerged from the haze. Maya, a brilliant astrophysicist, piloted the ship.

"Unknown spacecraft, identify yourself!" Jack hailed.

"This is Maya, astrophysicist on board the Aurora. And you are...?" Maya replied, her voice melodious.

"Jack, explorer on the Starblade. Nice to meet you, Maya."

As Jack and Maya communicated, their initial wariness gave way to curiosity.

"I've never seen a ship like yours," Jack said, impressed.

"Thanks! I designed it myself. What brings you to these skies?" Maya asked, her eyes sparkling.

"Just exploring. I've never met an astrophysicist before," Jack replied.

Maya laughed. "Well, now you have."

Their ships docked, and Jack boarded the Aurora. Maya welcomed him with a warm smile.

"Welcome aboard," Maya said.

"Thanks. Your ship's amazing," Jack said, looking around.

Maya smiled. "Glad you like it."

As they walked, their hands touched, sparking a connection.

Maya shared her research with Jack, revealing hidden patterns in the universe.

"Your research is fascinating," Jack said, reading Maya's notes.

"Thanks! I'm trying to unlock dark matter's secrets," Maya explained.

"You're passionate about it," Jack observed.

Maya's eyes shone. "I am. It's like unraveling the universe's mysteries." As they delved deeper into each other's lives, Jack's troubled past surfaced.

"Jack, what's wrong?" Maya asked, sensing his turmoil.

"Just demons from my past," Jack replied, his voice heavy.

Maya's compassion enveloped him. "I'm here for you, Jack."

Together, they ventured into the heart of the nebula, witnessing breathtaking wonders.

"Look! A nebula nursery," Maya exclaimed.

"Breath-taking," Jack whispered, awestruck.

As they explored, their love blossomed.

Duty called, forcing Jack and Maya apart.

"I have to go," Jack said, his voice heavy.

Maya's eyes welled up. "When will I see you again?"

"Soon. I promise," Jack reassured her.

Maya discovered a wormhole, leading her to Jack's memories.

"Jack's memories are flooding my mind," Maya said, amazed.

"You're experiencing his past?" Jack asked.

Maya nodded. "Our connection is deeper than I thought."

Reunited, their love ignited like a supernova.

"Maya, I've missed you," Jack said, embracing her.

"I've missed you too, Jack," Maya replied.

Their love burned brighter than any star.

As they approached the event horizon of a black hole, Jack and Maya realized their love knew no bounds.

"As we approach the event horizon...," Jack began.

"Our love will transcend space and time," Maya finished.

Together, they crossed into the unknown, forever entwined...

Chapter 1 - McGregor Ranch

The old mansion had been abandoned for decades, its grandeur and beauty slowly being consumed by the passing of time. But it was not entirely empty. A dark presence lurked within its walls, waiting for the perfect moment to strike. When a group of friends decided to explore the mysterious mansion, they uncovered a web of secrets and lies that led them down a terrifying path. As they delved deeper into the heart of the mansion, they began to experience strange and unexplainable occurrences that threatened to tear them apart.

As the night wore on, the group discovered that the mansion was home to a malevolent spirit, one that had been awakened by their presence. The spirit, born from a dark history of murder and betrayal, began to manipulate and toy with the group, leading them further into the depths of madness and terror. With each passing moment, the group realized that they had to uncover the secrets of the mansion and put an end to the spirit's reign of terror before it was too late. But as they searched for answers, they began to question their own sanity and wondered if they would ever make it out alive.

Chapter 2 - Venturing Deeper

The group encountered a series of eerie and unexplained occurrences. Doors creaked open and shut on their own, and disembodied whispers seemed to follow them wherever they went. Emily, a petite and reserved psychology student, began to feel an intense sense of dread, as if something was watching her every move. Matt, a rugged and skeptical history major, dismissed the strange happenings as mere hallucinations, but even he couldn't shake off the feeling of being trapped in a living nightmare.

Their group consisted of five friends, each with their own unique skills and motivations. There was Sarah, a thrill-seeking journalist, always on the lookout for the next big story; Jake, a tech-savvy engineer, who had brought along an array of ghost-hunting gadgets; and Chris, a quiet and introspective philosophy major, who seemed to sense the presence of something malevolent lurking in the shadows. Together, they had decided to explore the mansion, hoping to uncover its dark secrets and perhaps even capture some evidence of the paranormal.

As they explored the dusty and cobweb-covered rooms, they stumbled upon a hidden diary belonging to a former occupant, a young woman named Elizabeth. The diary revealed a tragic tale of love, loss, and betrayal, which seemed to be connected to the malevolent spirit they had encountered. Elizabeth had lived in the mansion with her husband, Malcolm, a wealthy and influential man, who had been involved in some shady dealings. Their marriage had been marked by infidelity and violence, and Elizabeth's diary hinted at a dark and sinister force that had consumed them both.

The group realized that they had to uncover the truth behind Elizabeth's story if they wanted to survive the night. But as they delved deeper into the mystery, they began to experience strange and terrifying phenomena. Doors slammed shut, trapping them in rooms, and ghostly apparitions began to appear, their eyes black as coal. The group knew they had to work together if they wanted to uncover the secrets of the mansion and escape alive. But as the night wore on, they began to suspect that one of their own might be hiding a dark secret, one that could prove deadly.

Chapter 3 - A Hidden Room

As they continued to explore the mansion, they stumbled upon a hidden room deep in the basement. Inside, they found a series of ancient artifacts and relics, each one more sinister than the last. There was a taxidermy owl with glassy eyes, a collection of rusty surgical tools, and a leather-bound book adorned with strange symbols.

"This is some creepy stuff," Matt said, holding up the book. "What is this, some kind of occult ritual manual?"

"I don't know, but I don't like it," Emily replied, shuddering. "Let's get out of here."

But Sarah was intrigued. She began to flip through the pages of the book, her eyes scanning the strange symbols and diagrams.

"Guys, look at this," she said, her voice barely above a whisper. "This is a ritual for summoning a spirit. I think Elizabeth and Malcolm were involved in some kind of dark magic."

As she spoke, the lights in the room began to flicker, and the air grew colder. The group exchanged nervous glances, sensing that they were getting close to uncovering the truth.

But then, they heard a noise. Footsteps, heavy and deliberate, coming from the floor above.

"What was that?" Chris whispered, his eyes wide with fear.

"I don't know, but I don't like it," Jake replied, his hand on the camera slung around his neck.

The group hesitated, unsure of what to do next. But then, they heard the footsteps again, this time closer.

"I think we should get out of here," Emily said, her voice trembling.

But Sarah was frozen, her eyes fixed on the book in her hand.

"We can't leave now," she said, her voice barely above a whisper. "We have to uncover the truth."

As she spoke, the lights went out, plunging the room into darkness. The group was trapped, surrounded by the sinister artifacts and relics. And then, they heard the voice. Low and menacing, it seemed to come from all around them.

"Welcome to my home," it said. "You'll never leave."

Chapter 4: The Dark Secret

As the group tried to make sense of the eerie voice and the darkness surrounding them, they heard footsteps coming from the floor above. Heavy and deliberate, they seemed to be getting closer.

"Guys, we need to get out of here, now!" Emily whispered urgently. But Sarah hesitated, her eyes fixed on the book in her hand. "We can't leave yet. We have to uncover the truth."

Matt grabbed her arm. "Sarah, come on! We can't stay here."

But Sarah shook him off. "No, Matt. I think I've found something." As she spoke, the lights flickered back to life, revealing a hidden message scrawled on the wall. "Look," Sarah said, her voice trembling. "It's a warning."

The message read: "Beware the traitor among you."

The group exchanged nervous glances. Who could the traitor be?

Suddenly, Chris spoke up. "I think I know who it might be."

"Who?" Emily asked, her voice barely above a whisper.

Chris hesitated before answering. "I think it's Jake."

The group gasped in shock. Jake's eyes widened in protest. "What are you talking about, Chris?"

But Chris continued. "I saw you arguing with Malcolm's ghost earlier. What were you talking about?"

Jake's face turned red with anger. "That was nothing. Just a stupid misunderstanding."

But the group wasn't convinced. They began to question Jake, who grew more and more defensive.

As the tension escalated, the lights began to flicker again. The voice spoke once more. "You should have left when you had the chance."

And then, everything went black.

Chapter 5 - McGregor

As the group struggled to comprehend the darkness surrounding them, the malevolent spirit spoke again.

"Welcome, fools, to McGregor Ranch," it said, its voice dripping with malice. "A place where dreams come to die."

"Why do you haunt this place?" Sarah asked, her voice shaking.

"Because I am the legacy of Malcolm McGregor," the spirit replied. "A man consumed by ambition and greed. He built this ranch on blood and deceit, and now his darkness festers, infecting all who enter."

"What do you want from us?" Matt asked, trying to hide his fear.

"I want your souls," the spirit hissed. "To add to the collection of those who dared to trespass on McGregor land."

"But why?" Emily asked, her curiosity getting the better of her.

"Because McGregor Ranch is a nexus of darkness," the spirit explained. "A place where the veil between worlds is thin. And I am the guardian of that veil."

The group exchanged nervous glances. They knew they had to escape, but the spirit seemed to be everywhere, watching them.

"You'll never leave this place," it taunted. "For in McGregor Ranch, the living are not welcome."

As the spirit's laughter echoed through the halls, the group knew they had to act fast. They began to search for a way out, but every door led to more questions, more secrets, and more terrors.

And then, they stumbled upon an ancient diary belonging to Malcolm McGregor himself. As they flipped through its yellowed pages, they discovered a dark history of rituals, sacrifices, and forbidden knowledge.

"The truth is hidden in plain sight," Chris whispered, his eyes scanning the diary. "McGregor Ranch was built on an ancient burial ground. The spirits of the dead are restless, and Malcolm's darkness has awakened them."

The group knew they had to uncover the secrets of the diary if they wanted to survive. But as they delved deeper into the mysteries of McGregor Ranch, they realized that some secrets were better left unspoken.

Chapter 6 - Look Who's Laughing

Beneath the flickering candles, the group pored over the diary, unraveling the sinister threads of Malcolm's past. They discovered that he had made a pact with a malevolent entity, trading his soul for wealth and power.

As they read on, the air grew colder, the shadows twisting into grotesque forms. The spirit's presence loomed over them, its malevolent energy seeping into their pores.

Suddenly, Jake slammed the diary shut, his eyes wide with terror. "We have to get out of here, now!"

But it was too late. The spirit's laughter boomed through the room, and the candles extinguished, plunging them into darkness.

In the blackness, the group heard footsteps, heavy and deliberate, coming from the depths of the ranch. The spirit's voice whispered in their ears, "You should have left when you had the chance."

As they stumbled through the darkness, desperate to escape, they realized that McGregor Ranch was a labyrinth of terrors, designed to trap the living forever.

And then, they saw it: a door hidden behind a tattered tapestry, adorned with ancient symbols of protection. The spirit's voice sneered, "You think you can escape? I have been waiting for you."

With trembling hands, Sarah pushed open the door, revealing a narrow stairway leading down into the darkness. "This is our only chance," she whispered.

As they descended the stairs, the spirit's laughter echoed above, and the door slammed shut behind them, trapping them in the depths of McGregor Ranch.

In the darkness, they waited, frozen in terror, as the spirit's presence closed in around them...

Chapter 7 - Air Grew Colder

The group huddled together, their hearts racing, as they tried to make sense of their surroundings. They found themselves in a damp, dimly lit chamber, the walls lined with ancient artifacts and relics.

"This is some kind of twisted shrine," Matt whispered, his eyes scanning the room.

"Look," Emily said, pointing to a series of symbols etched into the wall. "These match the ones on the diary."

Sarah's eyes widened as she realized the connection. "This must be where Malcolm performed his dark rituals."

Suddenly, Chris spoke up, his voice trembling. "Guys, I think we're not alone down here."

As he spoke, the air grew colder, and the shadows seemed to twist and writhe on the walls. The group heard a faint whispering, a soft chanting that seemed to come from all around them.

"What's happening?" Jake asked, his voice barely above a whisper.

The whispering grew louder, more urgent, and the group felt a presence closing in around them.

"We have to get out of here," Matt said, his voice firm. "Now."

But as they turned to leave, they saw it. A figure, tall and imposing, standing in the shadows. Its eyes glowed with an otherworldly light, and its presence seemed to fill the room.

"Welcome to my domain," it said, its voice low and menacing. "You will never leave."

The group froze, paralyzed with fear, as the figure began to move towards them...

As the figure loomed closer, the group's fear turned to panic. In the chaos, they became separated.

Sarah and Emily found themselves alone, stumbling through the dark corridors of the ranch. They heard the sound of footsteps behind them, but didn't dare look back.

Chapter 8 - Keep Moving

"Keep moving," Sarah whispered, her hand grasping Emily's. "We have to find the others."

Meanwhile, Matt and Jake were trapped in a room filled with ancient artifacts. The figure had slammed the door shut, trapping them inside.

"We have to find a way out," Matt said, his eyes scanning the room frantically.

But Jake just shook his head. "We're not getting out of here alive."

Chris, alone and disoriented, stumbled through the darkness. He heard the whispering in his ear, tempting him with twisted promises.

"Join me," the voice whispered. "Together, we can unlock the secrets of McGregor Ranch."

Chris's heart raced as he tried to resist the voice. But it was getting harder to distinguish reality from illusion...

As for the figure, it continued its relentless pursuit of the group. Its presence seemed to be everywhere, its power growing stronger by the minute.

The group's only hope was to reunite and uncover the secrets of the ranch before it was too late. But as they navigated the treacherous corridors, they realized that some secrets were better left unspoken...

"Sarah, wait!" Emily screamed, but it was too late. The figure loomed over them, its eyes blazing with an otherworldly intensity. Sarah tried to run, but her feet felt heavy, as if rooted to the spot.

The figure reached out a bony hand and grasped Sarah's arm, its touch like ice. Emily watched in horror as Sarah's eyes turned black, her body contorting in ways that seemed impossible.

"NOOO!" Emily screamed, but her cry was drowned out by the sound of Sarah's bones snapping, her body crumbling to the ground.

Emily stumbled backward, tripping over her own feet. She fell hard onto the cold floor, the wind knocked out of her.

As she struggled to catch her breath, she saw Matt and Jake, their eyes frozen in terror, their bodies suspended in mid-air by some unseen force.

The figure began to whisper to them, its voice like a rusty gate, and they started to twist and contort, their bodies elongating like rubber.

Emily scrambled to her feet and ran, not stopping until she reached the front door of the ranch. She flung it open and stumbled out into the night, not stopping until she reached her car.

She drove away from the ranch, not looking back, the sound of her friends' screams echoing in her mind.

The next morning, the police found Emily, catatonic and alone, her car parked on the side of the road. She never spoke of that night, but the look in her eyes told a thousand horror stories.

The McGregor Ranch was left abandoned, its dark secrets buried within its crumbling walls. But some say that on certain nights, when the moon is full, you can still hear the screams of Sarah, Matt, and Jake, forever trapped in the ranch's labyrinthine corridors.

Chapter 9 - Emily

The McGregor Ranch claimed four lives that night, leaving only Emily to tell the tale... or not tell it!!

Laughter echoed through the sterile room as Emily's eyes darted around, her gaze never settling. Dr. Lee's calm voice attempted to soothe her.

"Emily, can you tell me what happened that night? What do you remember?"

Emily's voice trembled, her words spilling out in a rush. "I remember the darkness, the whispers. It was everywhere, in my head, around me. I saw Sarah, Matt, Jake... they were... they were twisted, contorted. Oh God, their eyes..."

Dr. Lee nodded, her expression empathetic. "Go on, Emily. What happened to them?"

Emily's voice dropped to a whisper. "The figure... it touched them, and they changed. Like they were made of clay, molded into something else. And the screams... I'll never forget the screams."

Dr. Lee scribbled notes on her pad. "And what about Chris? Do you know what happened to him?"

Emily's gaze drifted away, her eyes unfocused. "I don't know... I don't know if he's alive or dead. I just ran... I had to get out of there."

Dr. Lee's voice softened. "You're safe now, Emily. You're here, and I'm here to help you. Can you tell me more about the figure? What did it look like?"

Emily's laughter returned, a cold, mirthless sound. "It was... it was the darkness. It had eyes, but no face. And its touch... its touch was like ice."

Dr. Lee nodded, her expression thoughtful. "I see. And do you think this figure is still out there, watching you?"

Emily's eyes snapped back into focus, her voice barely above a whisper. "I know it is. I can feel it. Watching me, waiting for me."

Dr. Lee's expression turned grave. "Emily, I want you to know that you're safe here. We'll do everything to protect you. But I need you to understand that the events you described... they're not possible. They're a product of your trauma, your mind's way of processing the horror you experienced."

Emily's laughter grew louder, more hysterical. "You don't understand! It's real! I saw it, I felt it! It's still out there, waiting for me!"

Dr. Lee leaned forward, her voice firm but gentle. "Emily, listen to me. You're not alone. We'll get through this together. But you need to confront the reality of what happened. Your friends died in an accident, a tragic event. There's no figure, no darkness. It's just your mind's way of coping."

Emily's laughter stopped abruptly, her eyes flashing with anger. "You don't know anything! You weren't there! I know what I saw, what I felt. And I know it's still out there, waiting for me."

The session ended with Emily's words hanging in the air, a sense of unease settling over Dr. Lee. She couldn't shake the feeling that Emily was telling the truth, that something sinister lurked in the shadows, watching and waiting. But she pushed the thought aside, focusing on her duty to help Emily heal. Little did she know, the darkness was closer than she thought...

Chapter 10 - Dr. Lee

Emily's eyes pleaded with Dr. Lee, her voice laced with desperation. "You don't understand, I need to go back there. I need to face it."

Dr. Lee's expression remained skeptical. "Emily, we've discussed this. Going back to the ranch will only trigger more trauma. You're not ready."

Emily's face contorted in a mix of fear and determination. "I don't care about being ready! I need to go back. I need to confront it."

Dr. Lee leaned forward, her voice firm. "Emily, you're not thinking clearly. You're still experiencing PTSD symptoms. Going back there will only worsen your condition."

Emily's voice rose, her words tumbling out in a frantic rush. "You don't get it! I need to go back. I need to make it stop. The dreams, the visions... they won't stop until I face it."

Dr. Lee's expression softened, but her tone remained resolute. "Emily, I understand you're scared, but running back to the source of your trauma won't solve anything. We need to work through this in a safe, controlled environment."

Emily's face twisted in a snarl, her eyes blazing with a hysterical rage. "YOU DON'T UNDERSTAND! I NEED TO GO BACK! I NEED TO MAKE IT STOP!"

The room fell silent, Dr. Lee's eyes widening in alarm as Emily's outburst hung in the air. For a moment, it seemed like Emily's fragile grip on reality had snapped. Then, as suddenly as it began, the rage dissipated, leaving Emily gasping for breath, her eyes welling up with tears.

Doctor's Notes

Patient: Emily
Session: 12
Observations: Emily's behavior has taken a disturbing turn. She's become increasingly agitated, demanding to return to the McGregor Ranch. Her eyes take on a wild, almost feral quality when discussing the topic.

Notable Quote: "McGregor is in my head. I can feel him. He's waiting for me."

Assessment: Emily's fixation on the ranch suggests a deep-seated psychological connection. I suspect she's experiencing some form of dissociation, possibly even identity fragmentation. The mention of "McGregor" being in her head implies a blurring of reality and fantasy.

Theory: Emily's trauma has created a mental construct, a manifestation of her fear and anxiety. This "McGregor" entity represents the darkness she experienced at the ranch. Her mind is attempting to process the horror by giving it a tangible form.

Concerns: Emily's growing instability raises concerns about her safety and the safety of those around her. If she continues to deteriorate, I fear she may become a danger to herself or others.

Next Steps: I'll continue to monitor Emily's progress, exploring the possibility of introducing anti-psychotic medication to stabilize her mental state. However, I fear we're running out of time. If Emily's condition worsens, more drastic measures may be necessary.

Dr. Lee leaned forward, her eyes locked on Emily's. "Tell me about McGregor, Emily. What does he look like to you?"

Emily's gaze drifted away, her voice barely above a whisper. "He's tall, imposing. His face is... twisted, like it's made of shadows. Eyes that burn with an otherworldly intensity. He's always watching, waiting."

Dr. Lee's expression remained neutral. "And what's his story, Emily? Why do you feel so connected to him?"

Emily's eyes snapped back into focus, her voice laced with a mix of fear and fascination. "McGregor was a rancher, a recluse. He made a pact with something dark, something ancient. It consumed him, body and soul. Now he's a vessel, a doorway to... to whatever is on the other side."

Dr. Lee scribbled notes on her pad. "And you feel like he's still out there, waiting for you?"

Emily nodded, her voice trembling. "Yes. He's patient, calculating. He knows I'll come back to the ranch eventually. And when I do... he'll be waiting."

Dr. Lee's gaze locked onto Emily's, her expression softening. "Emily, we'll work through this. We'll unravel the mystery of McGregor and the ranch. But you need to understand, it's not real. It's a manifestation of your trauma, your fear."

Emily's laughter was a cold, mirthless sound. "You don't understand, Doctor. McGregor is real. And he's coming for me."

Chapter 11 – Think of it Like a Prism

Dr. Lee leaned forward, her eyes locked on Emily's. "You see, Emily, our reality is shaped by our experiences, our beliefs, and our perceptions. What we think is real can be influenced by many factors."

Emily's gaze remained fixed on the floor, her expression skeptical.

Dr. Lee continued, "Think of it like a prism. Light passes through, and it's refracted into different colors, different perspectives. Our minds work in a similar way. We take in information, and our brain processes it, creating our reality."

Emily's eyes narrowed, her voice barely above a whisper. "So, you're saying McGregor isn't real?"

Dr. Lee's expression turned gentle. "I'm saying that McGregor represents something real to you, Emily. A manifestation of your fear, your trauma. But the McGregor you see, the one in your mind, that's a product of your perspective."

Emily's gaze lifted, her eyes searching Dr. Lee's face. "And what about the others? Sarah, Matt, Jake... did they see him too?"

Dr. Lee's voice softened. "Their perspectives, their realities, were likely different from yours. But that doesn't mean their experiences weren't real to them."

Emily's eyes dropped, her voice laced with doubt. "I don't know what's real anymore."

Dr. Lee's hand reached out, her touch gentle on Emily's arm. "That's okay, Emily. We'll work through this together. We'll explore your perspective, and we'll find a way to heal."

Dr. Lee's expression turned thoughtful, her eyes never leaving Emily's face. "You see, Emily, our reality is shaped by our experiences, our beliefs, and our perceptions. What we think is real can be influenced by many factors."

Emily's gaze remained fixed on the floor, her expression skeptical. "So, you're saying my mind is playing tricks on me?"

Dr. Lee leaned forward, her voice taking on a gentle quality. "Not tricks, Emily. More like... interpretations. Your mind is trying to make sense of what happened at the ranch. It's creating a narrative to help you cope."

Emily's eyes narrowed, her voice laced with doubt. "But what about the things I saw? The shadows, the eyes... McGregor?"

Dr. Lee's expression turned empathetic. "Those are symptoms of your trauma, Emily. Your mind is processing the horror you experienced, and it's manifesting in these... visions."

Emily's gaze lifted, her eyes searching Dr. Lee's face. "And what about the others? Sarah, Matt, Jake... did they see him too?"

Dr. Lee's voice softened. "Their experiences, their perceptions... they're all unique, Emily. But that doesn't mean their reality is any less real to them."

The air seemed to thicken, heavy with the weight of Emily's doubts and fears. And then, like a whispered promise...

Emily's eyes widened, her face pale. "No, no, no... this can't be happening. I'm not crazy, I know what I saw!"

Dr. Lee's expression turned calm, soothing. "Emily, please..."

But Emily was beyond consolation. She leapt from the couch, her voice rising to a hysterical pitch. "You don't understand! McGregor is real! He's waiting for me!"

Dr. Lee stood, her hands outstretched. "Emily, calm down..."

But Emily was beyond reason. She paced the room, her eyes wild. "I won't let him win! I won't let him consume me!"

Dr. Lee's voice turned firm. "Emily, stop. You're going to hurt yourself."

Emily's pacing halted, her chest heaving. And then, in a voice barely above a whisper... "I'll go back. I'll go back to the ranch, and I'll face him."

Dr. Lee's expression turned grave. "Emily, I'm going to have to consult with Dr. Patel."

Emily's eyes narrowed. "Who's that?"

Dr. Lee hesitated. "Dr. Patel is... the creator of the Quantum Core. A machine capable of manipulating time and space."

Emily's eyes widened. "Time travel?"

Dr. Lee nodded. "Yes, Emily. I think it's time we explored... unconventional options."

The room seemed to spin around Emily, her mind reeling with the implications. And then, like a whispered promise... the sparkles returned, swirling around her in a maddening dance.

Chapter 12 - FaceTime

Dr. Lee stepped away, her eyes locked on the screen as she initiated the FaceTime call. Dr. Sofia Patel's face appeared, her dark hair pulled back in a sleek ponytail, her brown eyes warm with concern.

"Ruining, what's the situation?" Dr. Patel asked, her voice crisp and authoritative.

Dr. Lee's expression turned grave. "Sofia, it's Emily. She's deteriorating rapidly. The trauma from the ranch is manifesting in... unusual ways."

Dr. Patel's eyebrows furrowed, her eyes narrowing. "Unusual ways?"

Dr. Lee hesitated. "She's seeing things, Sofia. A figure, McGregor. She's convinced he's real, waiting for her."

Dr. Patel's expression turned thoughtful, her lips pursed. "I see. And you think the Quantum Core can help?"

Dr. Lee nodded, her eyes locked on the screen. "I do, Sofia. We need to explore every option. Emily's running out of time."

Dr. Patel's face turned resolute, her jaw set. "Agreed. I'll start running simulations. But Ruining, we need to be cautious. The Quantum Core is still experimental. We can't predict the consequences."

Dr. Lee's expression turned somber, her eyes clouded with worry. "I know, Sofia. But what choice do we have? Emily's slipping away from us."

Dr. Patel's face softened, her eyes filled with empathy. "We'll do everything we can, Ruining. We'll bring Emily back."

The screen flickered, and Dr. Patel's face disappeared, leaving Dr. Lee to ponder the uncertain road ahead.

Dr. Lee escorted Emily to the private jet, its engines humming in the distance. Emily's eyes were sunken, her face pale, as she gazed out at the aircraft.

"We're going to Dallas, Emily," Dr. Lee explained, her voice gentle. "Dr. Patel is waiting for us. She's going to help you."

Emily nodded, her expression vacant, as she boarded the plane. Dr. Lee followed, her eyes never leaving Emily's face.

The flight was smooth, the skies clear, as they soared over the heartland of America. Emily sat silently, her eyes fixed on point beyond the horizon, while Dr. Lee worked on her laptop, her brow furrowed in concentration.

As they began their descent into Dallas, Emily stirred, her gaze drifting back to Dr. Lee. "Where are we?" she asked, her voice barely above a whisper.

Dr. Lee smiled reassuringly. "We're in Dallas, Emily. Dr. Patel is waiting for us."

The plane touched down, and Dr. Lee escorted Emily to a waiting car, its engine purring softly. They glided through the city streets, the Texas sun beating down upon them, until they arrived at a sleek, modern building, adorned with the logo "NeuroSphere Innovations".

Dr. Patel greeted them warmly, her eyes shining with compassion, as she enveloped Emily in a gentle hug. "Welcome, Emily. We're going to help you."

Emily's expression remained numb, her eyes vacant, as Dr. Patel led her into the heart of the facility, where the Quantum Core waited, its secrets and mysteries ready to be unlocked.

Chapter 13 - "NeuroSphere Innovations"

Dr. Lee and Dr. Patel stood outside the Quantum Core chamber, their faces grave with concern, as they brainstormed the potential outcomes of putting Emily through the experimental treatment.

"If we succeed," Dr. Patel began, her voice measured, "we could potentially reset Emily's timeline, erasing the trauma she experienced at the ranch."

Dr. Lee nodded, her eyes narrowed in thought. "But what if we create a paradox? What if Emily's actions in the past alter the present in unforeseen ways?"

Dr. Patel's expression turned somber. "We risk creating a butterfly effect. Small changes with catastrophic consequences."

Dr. Lee's voice dropped to a whisper. "And what if Emily becomes trapped in the loop? Reliving the same trauma over and over..."

Dr. Patel's face set in determination. "We'll monitor her closely. We'll be ready to pull her out if anything goes wrong."

Dr. Lee's eyes locked onto Dr. Patel's. "Are we playing God, Sofia? Tampering with the fabric of time?"

Dr. Patel's expression turned resolute. "We're giving Emily a chance to heal. To escape the hell she's living in."

The silence that followed was heavy with the weight of their decision, as they steeled themselves for the unknown consequences of their actions.

As the machines hummed to life, Dr. Lee and Dr. Patel stood anxiously beside Emily, who lay motionless on the Quantum Core chamber's sleek, silver table. The word "MERGING" flashed ominously on the screen above, in eerie, pulsing letters that seemed to writhe like living shadows.

"Initiating quantum entanglement," a robotic voice intoned, as a latticework of laser beams enveloped Emily's fragile form.

Dr. Lee's eyes locked onto Dr. Patel's, her face pale with trepidation. "What have we done, Sofia?"

Dr. Patel's jaw clenched, her voice firm. "We're giving Emily a second chance."

The machines reached a fever pitch, the air electric with anticipation. The word "MERGING" pulsed faster, its letters twisting into grotesque, macabre grins.

Suddenly, Emily's body arched, her eyes snapping open with a jolt. A blood-curdling scream tore from her lips, as the Quantum Core's energies surged to a blinding crescendo.

Chapter 14 - Emerging Sunshine

As Emily emerged from the shimmering portal of the Noshe, she found herself on a planet bathed in an ethereal, iridescent glow. The air vibrated with an otherworldly energy, and the ground beneath her feet hummed with a gentle, pulsing light.

Before her lay a vast, crystalline plain, stretching towards a horizon that seemed to curve into infinity. And there, scattered across the plain like delicate, glowing petals, sat a gathering of spiritual beings.

Each being was shrouded in a soft, luminescent aura, their faces serene and their eyes closed in deep meditation. The air around them rippled with gentle, shimmering waves, as if the very fabric of reality was being woven and unwoven with each breath.

Emily wandered through the gathering, her footsteps quiet on the crystal ground. She felt a deep sense of peace settle over her, as if she had stumbled into a dream she had always known, but never remembered.

One of the beings, an ancient, wispy form with eyes like starlight, opened its gaze to meet hers. "Welcome, traveler," it whispered, its voice like a breeze through the cosmos. "We have been waiting for you. We will guide you through the realms of the soul, and show you the secrets of the universe."

The Monk's gentle smile broadened, his eyes twinkling like celestial bodies. "You are far, far away from Dallas, child. You have transcended the bounds of space and time. Here, in this realm, all your troubles, all your fears, all your doubts are but a distant memory."

Emily's gaze wandered, taking in the surreal beauty of the crystalline plain, the shimmering auras of the meditating beings, and the infinite horizon that seemed to stretch into the very fabric of existence. A sense of wonder, of awe, began to dawn on her.

"But...how?" she whispered, her voice barely audible over the hum of the planet's energy.

The Monk's chuckle was like a soft breeze on a summer's day. "The Noshe has brought you here, Emily. You have been chosen to receive a great gift, a gift of knowledge, of understanding, of peace."

As he spoke, a warm, golden light began to emanate from his form, enveloping Emily in its radiance. She felt a weight lifting, a burden she had carried for so long, slowly rising from her shoulders.

"Sunshine," the Monk whispered, his voice full of gentle joy. "You are bathed in the light of the cosmos. Let it fill you, let it heal you, let it set you free."

And as Emily basked in the golden glow, she felt her very essence begin to shift, to expand, to merge with the infinite expanse of the universe. She was no longer just a woman from Dallas, with problems and fears and doubts. She was becoming something more, something greater, something eternal.

The Monk's eyes sparkled with delight, his smile radiant with warmth. "Ah, Sunshyne, my child, I shall teach you the ways of the cosmos, the secrets of the universe, and the mysteries of the soul."

With a gentle gesture, he beckoned her to follow him, and Sunshyne rose, her feet bare, her heart full of wonder. Together, they walked across the crystalline plain, the meditating beings parting like a sea of light to let them pass.

They reached a shimmering pool of water, its surface reflecting the infinite horizon like a mirror. The Monk turned to Sunshyne, his eyes aglow with ancient wisdom.

"Look into the pool, Sunshyne, and see the truth of your soul. See the light that shines within you, the light that connects you to all that is, all that was, and all that will be."

Sunshyne peered into the pool, and as she gazed, her vision expanded, her consciousness unfolding like a lotus flower. She saw herself as a thread in the cosmic tapestry, connected to every star, every planet, every being in the universe.

The Monk's voice whispered in her mind, "You are Sunshine, a ray of light in the grand symphony of existence. You are a droplet of dew on the leaf of life, reflecting the beauty of the world."

As Sunshyne gazed deeper, she saw the secrets of the universe unfolding before her, like a scroll of golden light. She saw the mysteries of birth and death, of time and space, of love and laughter. And she knew, in that moment, that she was one with all, that she was Sunshine, eternal and infinite.

As Sunshyne basked in the radiance of this revelation, the Monk's whispery voice continued to guide her on her journey of self-discovery.

"Sunshine, you are the melody that harmonizes the discordant notes of life. Your essence is woven into the tapestry of existence, connecting all threads, past, present, and future. You are the gentle breeze that rustles the leaves of forgotten memories, awakening the scent of nostalgia."

As the Monk's words painted vivid images in her mind, Sunshyne's vision expanded, transcending the boundaries of time and space. She witnessed the cosmic dance of stars and galaxies, the symphony of atoms and molecules, and the celestial rhythm of life itself.

In this vast expanse, Sunshyne saw herself as a shimmering droplet of dew, reflecting the infinite beauty of the universe. Her consciousness merged with the essence of all beings, and she felt the pulse of creation coursing through her veins.

"Who am I?" she asked the Monk, her voice barely above a whisper.

The Monk's response echoed within her: "You are Sunshine, the embodiment of light, love, and laughter. You are the bridge between the finite and the infinite, the manifestation of the divine in every moment."

Sunshyne's heart swelled with an overwhelming sense of unity and belonging. Tears of joy streamed down her face as she realized that she was never separate, never alone. In this epiphanic moment, she knew that she was an integral part of the grand symphony, playing her unique note in perfect harmony with the universe.

The Monk's voice faded into the silence, leaving Sunshyne bathed in the warm glow of her newfound understanding. As she opened her eyes, the world around her transformed, revealing the hidden beauty and interconnectedness of all things.

From that moment on, Sunshyne walked in the light of her true nature, spreading warmth, compassion, and radiance wherever she went, illuminating the path for those seeking their own inner Sunshine. As Sunshyne gazed out into the cosmic horizon, she sensed Maya's presence, like a gentle ripple on the fabric of space-time. The stars seemed to twinkle in anticipation, their light dancing across the velvet expanse.

Suddenly, a shimmering aura materialized before her, taking the form of Maya. Her long, dark hair cascaded like a waterfall of night, framing a face that radiated an otherworldly glow.

Maya's eyes, pools of sapphire, locked onto Sunshyne's, and the two women felt the familiar jolt of their souls reconnecting. The air vibrated with the hum of their entwined energies.

"Sunshine," Maya whispered, her voice carried on the solar wind. "Our paths converge once more."

Sunshyne's heart swelled, and she opened her arms, embracing Maya's ethereal form. "Sister of the cosmos," she replied, "I've awaited your return."

As they merged, their essences swirling like celestial bodies, Sunshyne felt the secrets of the universe unfolding further. Maya's presence illuminated hidden pathways, revealing the mysteries of the multiverse.

Together, they rode the cosmic currents, their consciousness soaring on the wings of stardust and moonbeams. They danced among nebulae, their laughter echoing through the expanse, creating new stars with every step.

In this realm, time lost meaning. Eons condensed into moments, and moments expanded into eons. Sunshyne and Maya traversed realities, witnessing the birth and demise of galaxies, the evolution of life, and the eternal cycle of creation.

Their journey carried them to the Event Horizon, where the fabric of reality warped and bent. There, they found the Guardians of the Threshold, ancient beings tasked with safeguarding the secrets of the cosmos.

The Guardians regarded Sunshyne and Maya with an unblinking gaze, their eyes burning with an inner fire. "Why have you returned?" they asked, their voices like the rumble of black holes.

Maya's smile illuminated the darkness. "We come bearing the gift of Sunshine, the embodiment of light and love."

The Guardians nodded, their forms shifting like sand dunes. "Then let Sunshine's radiance illuminate the shadows. Let her presence awaken the dormant harmonies of the universe."

With the Guardians' blessing, Sunshyne and Maya embarked on a new odyssey, their footsteps resonating across the cosmos, leaving trails of stardust and wonder in their wake.

Their journey had just begun, for in a universe of endless possibilities, Sunshine's light would forever be the guiding force.

Chapter 15- Event Horizon

As they crossed the event horizon, the universe around them dissolved into a kaleidoscope of colors. Time warped and distorted, stretching into infinity.

"Forever entwined," Jack whispered, his voice barely audible over the cosmic din.

Maya snuggled closer, her head against his shoulder. "We'll dance among the stars, Jack. Together, we'll create our own universe."

"Do you think we'll find a way out?" Jack asked, his brow furrowed in concern.

Maya's laughter echoed through the void. "Does it matter? We're together. Our love will create its own reality." She wrapped her arms around him, holding tight.

"In every dimension, in every reality," Jack echoed, his voice filled with conviction.

As the black hole's gravity pulled them deeper, Maya's grip on Jack tightened. "I'm scared," she whispered.

Jack's arms enveloped her, pulling her close. "I've got you, Maya. We're in this together."

The darkness around them transformed into a radiant aura, enveloping them in warmth.

"Look!" Maya exclaimed, pointing to a nebula unfolding before them.

Jack turned, his cheek brushing against hers. "A celestial garden, blossoming with stars."

Maya's fingers intertwined with his. "Beauty born from chaos. Our love is the catalyst."

Within the heart of the singularity, they found a realm where space and time converged. Stars and galaxies swirled around them like fireflies in a cosmic dance.

"Where are we?" Jack asked, his voice filled with wonder.

Maya leaned back, her hands still clasped in his. "Everywhere. And nowhere. We're beyond the boundaries of space and time."

Jack's smile spread across his face. "Infinite possibilities."

Maya's face lit up with excitement. "We can explore them all, together."

As they drifted through the cosmos, their bodies swayed in harmony, their love shining brighter than any star.

As they floated through space, Jack thought back to their first meeting. "Hey, Maya, remember that college lecture where we met?"

Maya smiled. "You corrected my notes and I thought you were kind of full of yourself."

Jack laughed. "Yeah, but you liked me anyway."

Just then, a nearby star exploded in a brilliant display of light.

"Wow!" Jack exclaimed. "The universe is amazing!"

Maya's eyes sparkled. "And full of secrets waiting to be discovered. Can you imagine what we'll find together?"

As they floated, their love kept them grounded. A mysterious being from a nearby cloud approached.

"Greetings," it said. "Your love has changed the universe."

Jack and Maya exchanged amazed glances. "What do you mean?" Jack asked.

The being explained, "Your love has opened up new possibilities. You're the starting point for a whole new universe."

Maya squeezed Jack's hand. "What's our role in this new universe?"

The being's form shifted, like dust rearranging itself. "You'll shape the universe, guiding growth and change. Your love will be its foundation."

Jack's eyes locked onto Maya's. "Together, forever."

Maya beamed. "We'll create a universe where love comes first."

With the mysterious being guiding them, they set out to shape the universe, their love leading the way.

Chapter 16 - Drifting

As they floated through the cosmos, Jack and Maya faced a daunting problem: drifting apart.

"We need to find a way to stay together," Jack said, his voice urgent.

Maya nodded. "We can't keep drifting. We'll lose each other in the vastness of space."

Suddenly, a sleek spacecraft materialized around them. The hull shimmered, solidifying into a sturdy vessel.

"Welcome home, Jack and Maya!" Sunshine's warm voice filled the air.

Jack and Maya exchanged amazed glances.

"Sunshine! You're here!" Maya exclaimed.

"I've always been with you," Sunshine replied. "Now, let's get you two safe and sound inside Odyssey, your new home."

The spacecraft's interior transformed into a cozy living space. Jack and Maya settled into comfortable seats, grasping hands.

"Where are we headed, Sunshine?" Jack asked.

"Course plotted for the Andromeda Galaxy," Sunshine responded. "A beautiful destination for exploration and discovery."

As Odyssey soared through space, Jack and Maya gazed out the viewport, watching stars and galaxies unfold.

"We did it," Maya whispered, her eyes shining.

Jack smiled. "Together, forever."

Sunshine's gentle hum filled the background, a reassuring reminder of their newfound security.

Their journey had just begun, with the universe waiting to be explored. Jack: "Whoa, look at that! We're coming out of the wormhole."

Maya: "Finally! I was starting to think we'd never make it."

Sunshine (over comms): "Welcome to Elysium, Jack and Maya. Prepare for landing."

Jack: "Elysium? Sounds like a myth."

Maya: "Maybe it is. But look at that view!"

Odyssey touched down on Elysium's surface. Jack and Maya stepped out, gazing at the shimmering landscape.

Maya: "This is incredible. Like nothing I've ever seen."

Jack: "I know, right? The crystals are singing."

Maya: "You hear it too? It's beautiful."

Sunshine: "Elysium's energy signature is unique. It's responding to your presence."

Jack: "Our presence? What do you mean?"

Sunshine: "Your love, Jack. It's resonating with Elysium's frequency."

Maya: "That's amazing. Our love is harmonizing with the planet."

Jack: "And look at that heart-shaped star!"

Maya: "Our cosmic symbol. Let's explore."

As they ventured deeper into Elysium:

Maya: "This lake is stunning. What's that sparkling stuff?"

Jack: "Stardust, I think. From the crystal stars."

Maya: "Incredible. And the scent...it's like love."

Jack: "Smells like home to me."

Sunshine interrupted:

Sunshine: "Energy source detected. Follow me."

They approached a glowing portal.

Jack: "Ready?"

Maya: "Always."

"We're not just creating life," Jack realized. "We're rebirthing the cosmos."

Chapter 17 - Elysium

As they ventured deeper into Elysium, Jack and Maya stumbled upon the Crystal Caves of Aethoria. The entrance, a shimmering archway, beckoned them to explore the ancient secrets within. With each step, the crystals resonated with their love, illuminating hidden patterns and mysterious symbols.

Maya's eyes sparkled as she deciphered the ancient language. "This is incredible, Jack! Elysium's crystals hold the universe's history – and our love is the key to unlocking it." Together, they unraveled the mysteries, their love igniting the crystals.

Next, they navigated the shimmering waters of the Lake of Dreams, where stardust danced across the surface. Jack skipped stones, watching as ripples transformed into galaxies. "We're creating universes," Maya whispered, her voice filled with wonder.

As the sun dipped into Elysium's horizon, casting a warm, golden light, they arrived at the Temple of Unity. Its entrance pulsed with an energy that mirrored their love. "This is it," Jack said, his voice filled with awe. "The heart of Elysium."

Inside, they discovered a celestial map etched into the walls, revealing hidden pathways and unseen worlds. Maya's eyes widened. "This is the blueprint for the universe." Jack's fingers intertwined with hers. "And our love is the guiding force."

Their quest led them to the Peak of Infinity, where the cosmos unfolded before them like a tapestry. Jack and Maya stood at the edge of eternity, their love shining brighter than any star.

Suddenly, a celestial portal swirled to life, beckoning them to explore the unknown. "Ready for the next adventure?" Jack asked, his eyes burning with excitement.

Maya's smile illuminated the stars. "Always."

Together, they stepped through the portal and into the Celestial Realm of Arkeia. A realm of breathtaking beauty, where stars and galaxies converged in a cosmic dance.

A figure emerged from the celestial haze – an ethereal being, radiating pure light. "Welcome, Jack and Maya," the being said. "Your love has been chosen to unlock the secrets of Arkeia."

With those words, their journey through the realm began. They soared through nebulae, witnessing the birth of stars. They walked among galaxies, feeling the pulse of the cosmos.

Their love guided them, illuminating hidden truths and unseen wonders. And with each step, their bond grew stronger, resonating with the very fabric of the universe.

As they explored Arkeia, they discovered an ancient prophecy – one that foretold of their love and its power to shape the cosmos.

"The Prophecy of Elysium," Maya whispered, her eyes shining with awe.

Jack's arm wrapped around her, his voice filled with determination. "We'll fulfill it, together."

Their love had become the guiding force, shaping the destiny of the universe. And as they stood in the heart of Arkeia, they knew that their As they ventured into the heart of Elysium, the crystal formations surrounding them shimmered with an ethereal light, casting a kaleidoscope of colors across the terrain. The air vibrated with an otherworldly energy, resonating through every molecule.

The Crystal Caves of Aethoria unfolded before them, a labyrinthine network of glittering caverns and iridescent grottos. Ancient symbols etched into the walls pulsed with a soft, blue light, guiding them deeper into the caves.

The Temple of Unity rose from the crystal-studded landscape, its architecture a masterful blend of celestial geometry and organic curves. The structure's surface shimmered with a mesh of fine, silver lines, like the delicate patterns on a butterfly's wing.

As they approached the temple, a swirling portal materialized, its rim pulsating with a vibrant, electric blue. The air around them rippled and distorted, as if reality itself was bending to accommodate the portal's presence.

Stepping through the shimmering gateway, they entered the Celestial Realm of Arkeia. Nebulae stretched out before them, vast, shimmering expanses of gas and dust. Stars burst forth, blazing with radiant light, as galaxies coalesced from the cosmic dust.

The Fractured Star of Andromeda loomed ahead, its surface etched with ancient scars, a testament to the cataclysmic forces that had shaped the cosmos. The star's fractured energy pulsed through the realm, a palpable, electric tension.

Arkeia's guardian, an ethereal being of pure light, greeted them. "Welcome, explorers. Your presence has been foretold."

Guided by the guardian, they traversed the Luminous Gardens of Elyria. Rare celestial blooms flowered, radiating stardust and filling the air with sweet, crystalline fragrances. Petals shimmered like stardust, leaves glowed with soft, luminescent light.

The Celestial River of Arkeia flowed through the gardens, its waters shimmering with cosmic energy. Ripples disturbed the surface, as if the river itself was alive, responding to their presence.

The Crystal Palace of Aethoria rose from the gardens, its facets reflecting the beauty of the cosmos. Ancient knowledge etched into the walls revealed:

The History of the Cosmos: Chronicles of star birth and galaxy formation.

The Secrets of Elysium: Hidden pathways and unseen worlds.

The Celestial Atlas: A glowing, crystal map of the universe.

Within the palace, they discovered:

The Chamber of Resonance: A room where cosmic harmonies converged, echoing through the chambers like a symphony of celestial music.

The Hall of Reflections: A mirror showing the soul's journey through time, its surface rippling with the memories of countless civilizations.

The Garden of Dreams: A realm where imagination shaped reality, where thoughts took form and substance.

As they explored, the Crystal Palace remained, a beacon of knowledge

The Chamber of Resonance hummed with an otherworldly energy, its walls lined with crystalline structures that amplified the cosmic harmonies. The air vibrated with the reverberations of a thousand distant suns, their songs blending into a celestial symphony.

Maya's footsteps echoed through the chamber, her presence stirring the resonant frequencies. The crystals responded, shifting their vibrational patterns to harmonize with her energy.

Jack's eyes widened as he witnessed the phenomenon. "This is incredible. The chamber is attuning itself to Maya's presence."

The guardian's voice whispered in their minds. "The Chamber of Resonance recognizes those who resonate with the cosmos."

Beyond the chamber, the Hall of Reflections beckoned. A vast, mirrored surface stretched before them, reflecting the soul's journey through time. Memories of countless civilizations rippled across its surface, whispers of love, loss, and triumph.

Maya's gaze wandered across the mirror, her eyes tracing the contours of forgotten histories. "This is the collective memory of the universe."

Jack's voice was barely above a whisper. "And we're part of it."

The Garden of Dreams unfolded before them, a realm where imagination shaped reality. Thoughts took form and substance, manifesting as vibrant, ethereal blooms.

Maya's thoughts blossomed into a radiant flower, its petals shimmering with stardust. Jack's imagination crafted a gleaming, crystalline spire, its facets reflecting the beauty of the cosmos.

Their creations merged, forming a breathtaking landscape of wonder. The garden responded, nurturing their imaginations with the essence of the cosmos.

As they explored, the Crystal Palace revealed more secrets:

The Library of the Ancients: Tomes of forbidden knowledge, holding the secrets of creation.

The Observatory of Eternity: A window into the infinite, revealing the mysteries of time and space.

The Sanctuary of the Cosmos: A sacred realm, where the essence of the universe converged.

Their journey continued, guided by the Crystal Palace's ancient wisdom. Through the infinite expanse of discovery and wonder.

Into the heart of the cosmos.

Where secrets awaited.

And mysteries unfolded.

The Library of the Ancients beckoned, its shelves lined with tomes bound in a material that shimmered like stardust. Maya's fingers trailed across the spines, sensing the forbidden knowledge within.

"The Secrets of Creation," Jack whispered, his eyes scanning the titles. "The Origins of the Cosmos."

Maya's gaze settled on a tome adorned with intricate, celestial patterns. "This one," she said, her voice barely above a whisper.

The book opened, revealing pages filled with cryptic symbols and illustrations of cosmic phenomena. As they read, the knowledge resonated within them, expanding their understanding of the universe.

Next, they entered the Observatory of Eternity, a vast, domed chamber filled with celestial instruments of unparalleled precision. The guardian's voice guided them, explaining the workings of the cosmos.

"The Dance of the Galaxies," Jack marveled, watching as stars and galaxies moved in harmony.

"The Rhythm of Time," Maya whispered, her fingers tracing the patterns etched into the observatory's walls.

Their journey continued, leading them to the Sanctuary of the Cosmos. A sacred realm, where the essence of the universe converged.

As they entered, a radiant light enveloped them, imbuing their souls with the cosmic energy. The sanctuary's heart pulsed with an otherworldly power, resonating with their very being.

"This is the source," Maya whispered, her eyes aglow.

"The cosmic nexus," Jack agreed, his voice filled with awe.

Their presence harmonized with the sanctuary's energy, expanding their consciousness. The universe unfolded before them, a tapestry of wonder.

And within the tapestry, a hidden thread awaited.

A thread leading to the Hidden Realm of Arkeia.

A realm of secrets.

A realm of wonder.

Their journey continued.

Chapter 18 - The book of Emily

As Jack and Maya explored the Sanctuary of the Cosmos, a vision unfolded before them. A vision of Emily, standing within the McGregor Ranch house.

Emily's eyes locked onto something beyond the physical realm. Her presence began to shimmer.

Dr. Patel and Dr. Lee stood beside her, their faces etched with concern.

"Emily, we're losing you," Dr. Patel whispered.

"No," Emily replied, her voice barely audible. "I'm finding myself."

The neuropore device hummed to life.

Dr. Lee's voice was urgent. "We must transcend her consciousness."

Dr. Patel nodded. "Into the sunshine."

The device pulsed.
Emily's presence began to dissolve.
Her essence merged with the sunlight.
Transcended.
Free.
Jack and Maya witnessed the scene.
"What happened to Emily?" Jack asked.
Maya's gaze remained on the vision. "She was transcended."
"By Dr. Patel and Dr. Lee," Jack added.
The vision faded.
Their attention returned to the sanctuary.
The cosmic nexus pulsed.
"Emily's journey continues," Maya whispered.
"Beyond the physical realm," Jack agreed.
Their understanding expanded.
The universe unfolded.
New paths revealed.
Their journey continued.
Through the infinite expanse.
Of discovery and wonder.
As they ventured deeper into the sanctuary, they discovered:
The Chamber of Transcendence: Where consciousness merged with the cosmos.
The Portal of Eternity: A gateway to infinite possibilities.
The Celestial Library: Holding the secrets of the universe.
And within the library.
A tome awaited.
The Book of Emily.
Holding the secrets.
Of her transcension.
And the mysteries.

Of the neuropore device. The Book of Emily lay open, its pages filled with cryptic symbols and illustrations of cosmic phenomena. Jack's eyes scanned the text, seeking answers.

"Emily's transcension was not an accident," Maya whispered, her gaze tracing the symbols.

"It was a calculated event," Jack agreed, his voice filled with determination.

Dr. Patel and Dr. Lee's faces appeared in the pages, their expressions revealing a hidden truth.

"They knew Emily's potential," Maya said.

"And they facilitated her transcension," Jack added.

The Book of Emily revealed more:

The Neuropore Device: A gateway to higher consciousness.

The Sunshine Protocol: A transcension method.

The Cosmic Nexus: A convergence of energies.

As they read, the sanctuary's energy resonated with their understanding.

The Chamber of Transcendence beckoned.

"Emily's journey continues," Maya whispered.

"Through the cosmic nexus," Jack agreed.

Their presence merged with the chamber's energy.

Consciousness expanded.

The universe unfolded.

New paths revealed.

Their journey continued.

Through the infinite expanse.

Of discovery and wonder.

Beyond the chamber, the Portal of Eternity awaited.

A gateway to infinite possibilities.

The portal's energy pulsed.

"Are you ready?" Jack asked.

Maya's gaze met his. "We were born ready."

Together, they stepped through the portal.
Into eternity.
Where time had no bounds.
And space was infinite.
Their consciousness merged with the cosmos.
Becoming one with the universe.
Infinite possibilities unfolded.
And within the infinity.
A new reality awaited.
A reality born from their journey.

Through the infinite expanse.As Jack and Maya traversed the infinite expanse, visions of McGregor Ranch unfolded before them. Emily's friends, laughing and joyful, until the demonic creature known as McGregor emerged.

McGregor's presence darkened the ranch, its malevolent energy suffocating. Emily's friends tried to flee, but McGregor's powers trapped them.

The visions revealed the horrors:

Sarah, consumed by an unseen force, her screams echoing through the night.

Matt, possessed by McGregor's dark energy, turning against his friends.

Lisa, tortured by visions of her deepest fears, driven to madness.

Emily, desperate to save her friends, confronted McGregor.

The creature's true form manifested: a twisted, humanoid figure with eyes burning with malevolent intent.

McGregor's voice, a cacophony of terror, echoed through Emily's mind.

"You will never escape."

Emily's determination fueled her resistance.

She discovered the neuropore device, a possible escape.

Dr. Patel and Dr. Lee, secretly working to transcend Emily's consciousness.
The sunshine protocol, a desperate attempt to save Emily.
McGregor's powers raged against them.
But Emily's spirit persevered.
Her transcension into sunshine, a triumph over the darkness.
The visions faded.
Jack and Maya understood the truth.
Emily's story was not just a mystery.
It was a testament to her courage.
In the face of unimaginable horror.
Their journey continued.
Through the infinite expanse.
Of discovery and truth.
The darkness of McGregor Ranch contrasted with the radiant sunshine Emily had become.
A symbol of hope.
In the depths of despair.
Their consciousness merged with the cosmos.
Infinite possibilities unfolded.
And within the infinity.
A new reality awaited.
A reality born from Emily's courage.
Where darkness was vanquished.
By the light of truth.
And the power of the human spirit.

Don't miss out!

Visit the website below and you can sign up to receive emails whenever Anthony Fontenot publishes a new book. There's no charge and no obligation.

https://books2read.com/r/B-A-STPNB-OYKIF

BOOKS 2 READ

Connecting independent readers to independent writers.

Did you love *"Cosmic Horizon Collection"*? Then you should read *Star Line Horizon* by Anthony Fontenot!

A Gripping Space Opera Adventure

In the vast expanse of the galaxy, Captain Deloy and his infamous pirate crew, Maverick's Revenge, embark on a daring mission to take down the Aurora Cosmic Federation's prized vessel, Aurora's Hope.

With cunning hacks, precision sabotage, and fearless boarding, Deloy's crew must outwit and outmaneuver the Federation's elite forces.

As tensions rise and allegiances blur, Deloy's pirates forge unlikely alliances, confront rival enemies and face impossible choices that threaten the very fabric of the galaxy.

Join the Maverick's Revenge on their perilous quest for supremacy in the lawless cosmos.

high-stakes adventure

Space Opera
Read more at www.tiktok.com/@a.cosmic.horizon.

About the Author

A born and raised Texan, Anthony Fontenot will usually introduce himself as "basically Hank Hill". The casual observer may note that he has a very nice beard, unlike his animated counterpart. He collects VHS tapes, specifically of the horror and sci-fi genres. He's worked a myriad of jobs, his favorite being part of the team at Ripley's Believe It Or Not!, as well as being a light and sound technition for local and touring major music artists. He currently makes his living as a security guard. He enjoys making art, going to concerts, and spending time with family and friends.

Read more at www.tiktok.com/@a.cosmic.horizon.

Milton Keynes UK
Ingram Content Group UK Ltd.
UKHW042000291124
451915UK00004B/324